50p -

The Last Smile

Pete Sawyer, hero of the *Stone Angel* series of novels, is a private investigator who's half-French, half-American, and totally sophisticated. After careers as a Chicago cop, a federal narc and a Senate investigator abroad he's in business for himself in France.

One night in December his partner, Fritz Donhoff is gunned down in a Parisian street. He's an old man and, as he fights for his life, Pete attempts to trace his killer. If its cold vengeance he's lost, for Fritz has crossed many paths in his long life, but the shooting may be linked to the case he left behind and so Pete takes it over.

Susan Kape, a beautiful but crippled oil heiress, is determined to make her mark in the international art world. Her best chance is to acquire the priceless contents of an Etruscan tomb. All she needs is $18 million and Pete's protection while she has the discovery authenticated in Italy.

Pete agrees to take on this task purely for the sake of tracing Fritz's would-be assassin. The position he finds himself in would have appealed to the Etruscans' love of complication and survival, although they would not have approved of the crude murderers he has to stalk.

An inspired and satisfying mystery.

THE LAST SMILE

Marvin Albert

MACMILLAN
LONDON

First published in the United States of America

First published in the United Kingdom 1989 by
MACMILLAN LONDON LIMITED
4 Little Essex Street London WC2R 3LF
and Basingstoke

Associated companies in Auckland, Delhi, Dublin, Gaborone,
Hamburg, Harare, Hong Kong, Johannesburg, Kuala Lumpur,
Lagos, Manzini, Melbourne, Mexico City, Nairobi, New York,
Singapore and Tokyo

ISBN 0-333-48432-0

A CIP catalogue record for this book is available from the British
Library

Printed in Great Britain
by The Camelot Press, Southampton

For Roger Martin
Thanks for the push

1

ON THE FIRST SATURDAY NIGHT IN DECEMBER AT A FEW minutes before midnight Fritz Donhoff—my friend, partner, and the closest to a father I've ever known—was shot down near the Place Maubert in Paris.

It was shortly after 1 A.M. when Commissaire Gojon of the Brigade de Recherche et d'Intervention learned about it. He phoned my house down on the Riviera and left a message on my answering machine.

Seven hours later he called again and left another message.

I didn't get either message until Sunday night, because the snow was packed deep and solid on the upper slopes of the Alpes Maritimes and I was off spending a weekend with Arlette Alfani in Valberg.

There are swankier ski centers than Valberg. But not close enough to the Côte d'Azur to drive to and from comfortably when you've only got a short weekend to spare. Arlette had a court appearance scheduled for Monday morning. She also had a couple cases to finish preparing for the senior partners of her law firm Sunday night. Valberg was little more than an hour from her apartment in Nice. Another fifteen minutes to my house near Monaco.

Anyway, I don't go to winter resorts to mingle with the jet set and compare wardrobe chic. I go to ski. At a height of

1

over five thousand feet, with some of its runs starting at seven thousand, Valberg was more than adequate for that.

And with a snow bunny as luscious as Arlette Alfani along, there were also those *après-ski* hours to consider. Long, lazy, lusty hours we didn't care to waste mingling with anyone but each other. Meals and wine delivered by room service and damn the expense, because between the skiing and *après-ski*-ing we were too bushed to crawl out of bed.

A freezing wind was hurling the beginnings of a snow and sleet storm through the mountains around Valberg when we left on Sunday afternoon. But the route from those heights in the direction of the coast descends with dramatic swiftness. We did the customary piecemeal striptease along the way. By the time we entered the Cians Gorges, only a short way out of Valberg, the air had warmed enough for us to toss hats and gloves in the backseat. Fifteen miles later we were almost down to sea level, shedding our sheepskin coats. Another thirty minutes and we had to stop to exchange boots and heavy stockings for rope-soled canvas espadrilles.

I drove us into Nice between palm trees nodding gently in a balmy breeze, with the setting sun casting a golden shimmer across a bright blue Mediterranean.

It was difficult to believe in winter down there. Unless you looked back, at the white peaks shouldering the northern sky. Or straight ahead, to where a long, low roll of dark cloud was forming along the sea horizon and moving toward southern France with a speed indicating something more than a genial breeze behind it.

Arlette's apartment was a couple blocks from the beach, behind that venerable queen of the Riviera hotels, the Negresco. "I can give you a few hours to finish your homework," I suggested when we reached her building, "then come back and take you out to dinner."

Good try but no sale. An emphatically negative shake of her lovely head. "I have to be wide awake and full of steam tomorrow."

"A friendly dinner with a good bottle of wine is just what you'll need after working late, to settle you down to a night's sleep."

Arlette quirked an elegant raven-black eyebrow at me. "If we have a late dinner together, we'll wind up still together at breakfast. And while we're wonderful together in many ways, Pierre-Ange, getting a full night of sleep is not one of them."

Lawyers get that disturbing habit of concentrating on petty facts over intrinsic sentiment. A professional failing.

But she allowed me to carry her bag inside and gave me the key to open her apartment door for her. Frenchwomen like to let a man feel manly. They've learned by age ten that it makes him more manageable than beating him at arm wrestling. They tend to consider a man another form of child, pleasant to have around if handled with sufficient fore-thought.

I put down the bag and gave her back the key, and we kissed good-bye. The kiss was gathering passion when Arlette broke it up with a sharp elbow in my ribs. Not hard enough to crack bone, but enough to end our clinch before her resolve crumbled.

I said, "Ouch."

Arlette said, "*Go*—or I'll hate myself in the morning."

I went. Frank Crowley's studio was in the Old Town quarter of Nice, on the minuscule Place du Jésus. Crow's wife, Nathalie, was off in the States handling a series of business meetings for her mother's fashion house. So I figured the chances were I'd find him at work.

He was there. Enlarging the last of a group of photographs for an exhibition of his work at the BNP in Monte Carlo. While he finished the job I wandered around looking at the blowups he'd already finished and pinned to the studio walls. They were all views of ancient Provençal villages. The abnormally strong contrasts of light and shadow in each created an effect that somehow heightened reality. The kind of pictures a Cézanne might have turned out if he'd used a camera instead of a paintbrush.

Crow didn't look or act like any Cézanne. Closer to a stocky, freckled version of John Wayne: that earthy, laid-back cool coupled with that coiled-spring physical sureness when sudden action was called for. It was difficult to reconcile the lazy toughness with the sensitivity revealed in his pictures. Unless you knew Crow very well.

I'd known him since we'd served in the same squad in Vietman. Years later he'd visited my place on the Côte d'Azur and gotten hooked on the area and on my friend Nathalie. A while later he'd also gotten hooked on photography and had sold his half of a computer partnership to try it full time. Lately a picture-postcard firm had begun buying his photos. They weren't paying the kind of money he'd earned in the computer business but it helped reassure him that his new profession wasn't just a hobby.

Crow pinned the last enlargement on the wall and waved a blunt hand at the rest. "What d'you think, Pete?"

"They're good."

He nodded, satisfied. He didn't need more elaborate praise, not from me.

It was dark outside when we left the studio. The cloud rolling in from the sea had become a low blanket over Nice. Not a star peeping through. And the wind was building, bringing cold and a smell of rain on the way. The kind of weather that would have the winter tourists grumbling about not having come all the way from Oslo or Philadelphia or Geneva for *this*.

We walked around the corner of the Prussian restaurant across from Crow's studio, went a few steps along Rué Droit, and turned into an Irish pub. The Old Town has been getting as international as the city's plush beachfront lately. It started when some humble entrepreneurs figured out that what they'd previously thought of as a seedy neighborhood might be re-garded by visiting foreigners as quaint. They also figured a lot of those foreigners might want to relax in places where they felt like they'd never left home.

But that night the rest of the crowd in the pub sounded solidly French. Not a single Irish voice raised in either song or protest against the prices.

Crow and I were starting on our second round of drinks when he asked me out of nowhere, "How many years has it been now since you and your wife broke up?"

"I'm not in a mood for painful conversations tonight," I told him.

"I was just wondering if you're thinking about marrying the delicious Arlette."

"Are you thinking of divorcing the delicious Nathalie?"

"Between friends," Crow growled softly, "answering a well-intentioned question with a nasty one can get a guy a busted nose."

"Friends," I informed him, "are people who know when to mind their own business."

"I seem to remember doing you a small favor once. In 'Nam, wasn't it? Something like saving your life? That *ought* to earn me some small extra privileges."

"Sure. How about a free dinner? I've got a pot of beef *daube* in the fridge, and a new stock of wine we can try out while it's heating up."

"You're on. I don't feel like going home to an empty bed until I'm ready to pass out."

Crow's Citroën followed my Peugeot east out of Nice and along the Lower Corniche to Cap d'Ail. We turned down the twisty private drive and parked in the carport behind my house.

The place had been old when my mother's father bought and restored it. That was the French side of my parentage. My American father had never gotten to know the house. Nor me, for that matter. He'd died before I was born. No way of being sure if he would have been pleased to know me; but when it came to the house he'd definitely missed something in his short life.

It was typical Provençal. Solid and comfortable. Built to age well. I had a deep affection for the place, based, like most of an adult's deep affections, on semisubmerged memories of childhood pleasures.

It was screened from the few neighboring houses by fruit trees and flowering bushes, with a vast sweep of the Mediterranean spread out below. The sound and smell of the sea, and the taste of its salt in the air, were as much part of the house for me as its stone walls and orange-tile roof. On the side overlooking the sea there was a wide brick patio, laid out under an olive tree gnarled by centuries of defying everything nature could throw at it. Beyond the olive tree a wooded slope led down to the cliff-sheltered cove where I'd learned to swim as a kid.

I still swam from there whenever the weather permitted. Which was much of the time, but not tonight. A steady drizzle was topping off the wind and cold when Crow and I arrived. Crow got busy preparing a fire in the living-room fireplace while I went to start our meal and uncork a bottle.

On the way I stopped in the study and switched over my telephone answering machine, turning up the volume so I could hear it from the kitchen.

The first message of interest was from Fritz Donhoff.

"Hello, Pierre-Ange," the familiar deep voice boomed from the machine. "It is Fritz, here, calling from Paris. Friday evening. Four minutes past eight."

That had been a few hours after I'd left for Valberg with Arlette.

"I hope you are well, my boy," he countered, "and that the weather there is kinder than it is up here. Beastly winter. Typical for Paris, of course. But I'm afraid I won't be able to visit with you down there at this point, after all."

That didn't surprise me. I had invited him to be my guest for a few weeks, and Fritz had said he'd consider it. He always said that, being a polite man who appreciated friendly invitations. But he seldom came, and when he did he never stayed more than a few days. I kept explaining that a person in his seventies should get his lungs cleaned out with fresh air a few times a year. Fritz always agreed in principle. But he was your immutable city man. He got restless in the country. Maybe it was his blood system screaming for the pollution it was addicted to after so many decades.

The next part of Fritz's message contained his latest excuse. "I've gotten involved in a new investigation, you see. One that is developing unexpected facets. Also an unexpected amount of legwork, and my aging legs are not taking this winter too well. I could use your help on this one, if you can tear yourself away from the mind-dulling pleasures of the countryside. Please call me when you return home, and I'll explain what it's about and why I need you. Thank you, my boy."

End of message.

Then came the two from Commissaire Gojon, telling me what had happened to Fritz some thirty hours later, on Saturday night.

2

"AGE SHOULD . . . WALK THOUGHTFUL ON THE SILENT, solemn shore . . . Of that vast ocean it must sail so soon."

Fritz Donhoff had come up with that one from Young's "Night Thoughts" a year back when we were trying to see which of us could remember more poetry quotations on any particular subject. It was a way to pass the time without falling asleep. We were sitting in a car waiting for a couple guys to come out of a building so we could tail them, together or separately. The wait was nearing the end of its second hour. I'd topped Fritz on the subject of Love and he had evened the score with Beauty, and we were into Death.

"I don't think either of us is going to come up empty on this one," I said finally. "Death seems to have inspired more poems than any other subject."

"Naturally," Fritz said. "Love and Beauty—those tend to be a preoccupation of youth. Unfortunately, poets spend so many more of their years growing old. And brooding about it." He smiled briefly. "Like aging detectives."

"Maybe permission to write poetry should be revoked the same year you get old enough for a driver's license," I suggested.

"It wouldn't be a bad idea. There is quite enough gloom around without dying poets weeping on the world's shoulders."

"Some of them manage to be fairly cheerful about it, though," I pointed out. "Whitman, for example."

Fritz made a sour face. "You mean his 'Come, lovely and soothing Death . . .'? I can only assume he wrote that somewhat like a frightened citizen trying to persuade an armed mugger that he sympathizes with the mugger's social motivations."

"Hoping he'll be treated more mercifully than previous victims."

Fritz nodded his broad silver-haired head. "*I'm* under no such illusions. When Death comes for *me*, my boy, I won't pretend it's not an ugly, vicious enemy. I'll fight it, every inch of the way, with any weapon I can dredge up."

I remembered that when I stood looking at him lying there in the intensive care room in Paris, with the life-fluid replacements dripping into his veins through tubing plugged into both arms. The emergency medical team at the Hôtel Dieu, that grim fortress of a hospital on the Ile de la Cité surrounded by the River Seine, had taken two bullets out of him. Blood loss and internal damage had been extensive. If he had any fight left I couldn't see it.

Hell, I told myself, of course I couldn't *see* it. Fritz would be waging his battle deep down inside—on his own ground. He would surface after he won it.

That's what I told myself. But what showed didn't look encouraging. He hadn't regained consciousness in the day and night since the ambulance team picked him out of the gutter on Rue de la Montagne Sainte Geneviève. His heavy figure had shrunk. The bones of his big hands and face were abnormally prominent. The plump bags under his eyes had deflated like shriveled balloons.

The lighting didn't help. I'd been able to snag a seat on the last night plane out of the Côte d'Azur airport to Paris. It was now half-past two in the morning and dark outside. A single lamp burned in the room. In its feeble glow Fritz's color was ghastly.

I reminded myself that it wasn't the first time in his life he'd been shot. But the last time he'd been fifty-four. Twenty years older meant twenty years less resilient. Even for a man of Fritz Donhoff's solid strength. Taking his wrist, I found the pulse and was looking at my watch when the nurse came in.

"I did that just a few minutes before you arrived," she told me. "He's checked every half hour. As I told you, he's doing better than we expected when they brought him in."

I kept my fingers on his pulse and my eyes on the second hand of my watch for another twenty seconds. Slow but steady. I didn't ask the nurse about his chances. That I already knew. At this point he could go either way.

I wondered how many others had stood on this exact spot, watching someone they loved hover between life and death, in all the years the Seine had flowed past the Hôtel Dieu de Cité.

"You'll have to leave now," the nurse said as I patted Fritz's hand and straightened. "You can stay in the waiting room. Or go and come back when visiting hours start at eight."

"I'll be back," I told her. It wasn't going to do anything for Fritz if I hung around the hospital. And it wouldn't help me find whoever had gunned him down.

The young detective on guard in the corridor had wide shoulders and small, cold eyes. A junior inspector from the BRI. Commissaire Gojon had assigned him to note the identities of Fritz's visitors, coupled with making sure whoever had shot him didn't get inside to finish the job.

"I'd like to look at whatever was in his pockets when he was brought in," I told him. The cops would have already gone through it, but they didn't know Fritz the way I did. There might be something that had meaning only for me.

I followed Gojon's inspector down the corridor to the nursing office. He unlocked a drawer and handed me an envelope. I spread its contents on a table.

Nothing that came out of the envelope gave me any information about the case Fritz was on. Three things were missing: Fritz's wallet, his ring of keys—and the little notebook he always carried.

The young inspector's cold eyes watched me put everything back in the envelope. He returned it to the drawer. I went down the stairway and out of the hospital.

Outside the entrance I stopped to take a corduroy cap from the side pocket of my tweed jacket. I put it on and turned up my jacket collar. It wasn't raining that night in Paris, but it was colder than the south and I had dressed for it before going to the airport. Solid shoes with thick rubber soles, flannel trousers, a turtleneck cashmere sweater under the jacket. I hadn't brought a bag along because my Paris apartment was stocked with clothes for all seasons. But I didn't care to contract the first stages of pneumonia before I got there.

It didn't come as much of a surprise when I spotted Commissaire Gojon behind the wheel of his car in front of the hospital, waiting for me.

He would have instructed his young inspector to call him whenever I showed up. Two-thirty in the morning didn't mean the middle of a deep sleep for Gojon. He had been sleeping in restless snatches ever since his wife and left him to become the mistress of a solidly married citizen with several children.

Gojon had asked me about that sleeping problem once, drawing on my longer experience at being divorced. I had advised him that only time could cure the problem, but that getting another woman to share his bed might help. Maybe it wouldn't get him more sleep, but it could make not sleeping less of a drag than lying there all by himself staring wide-eyed at a dark ceiling. If he hit lucky.

I didn't know if he had taken my advice. We weren't *that* close. I didn't know of anybody who was that close with Commissaire Jean-Claude Gojon. That could be the reason his wife had opted out. Or maybe not. People who get to feeling trapped in a formerly loving relationship can't always explain the real reasons, even to themselves. *My* ex-wife had come up with half a dozen. All valid. But mutually contradictory.

I walked to Gojon's car and settled into the front seat beside him.

3

Gojon turned toward me, resting an elbow on the back of the seat. A streetlamp that cast light across my face threw a shadow against his, making the lenses of his glasses as black as their rims. That wouldn't be happenstance. Not with Gojon.

"So," he began in a flat and almost gentle tone, "tell me what you know about what happened to your partner."

"Not one damn thing, Commissaire."

I always addressed him as "Commissaire." I'd done him several professional favors in the past, and so far he'd kept to himself a couple things that could have lost me my license to work as a private investigator in France. And we'd had that late and slightly sloshed evening when we had let it down enough to discuss the slings and arrows of newly unwed life. But none of that put us on a first-name basis. And calling him by just his last name wouldn't have sounded respectful.

Gojon was not a good man to treat with even a hint of disrespect. The Brigade d'Intervention is the toughest bunch of cops in France. Gojon didn't look like he belonged in an outfit like that. He would have seemed just right as a banking director. Which he could have been. He had the right family connections, education, and manner. But I had seen how other men in the Brigade acted around him. The way combat troops do around the very rare officer they've learned can

13

handle rougher stuff than they can, give and take. They called him Commissaire. So did I.

He said, "You must have *some* information for me, Sawyer." Gojon didn't have to treat me with equal respect. "For example, was Monsieur Donhoff working on something at the time he was shot?"

Monsieur Donhoff. Gojon had respect for Fritz: Fritz had been a police detective before Gojon was born. In addition to being something of a legend in Paris for his deadly accomplishments as a member of the city's anti-Nazi underground during the war.

"He was on a case," I told Gojon. "I don't know what or who or why." I told him about Fritz's phone message.

Gojon didn't like it. "That still doesn't tell me if the case contains the reason he was shot. It might simply be what it looks like. An armed robbery—with Monsieur Donhoff doing something that made the holdup man nervous enough to shoot. *Or* it could have been someone from the past with a grudge against him. There must be a number of those, going a long way back."

"The robbery was a fake." I told Gojon about the little notebook that should have been among Fritz's things. "A mugger wouldn't have any reason to take that along with the valuables. The same applies to any old enemy finally getting even. Fritz only used the book to jot down current stuff— that day's notes."

"You see," Gojon said, "you did know something."

"Have you had a look around Fritz's apartment?"

Gojon nodded, making the masklike shadow slide up his narrow patrician face and then back down. "But someone else got in there ahead of us. Perhaps the one who stole his keys. Again, it appeared to be a simple burglary."

"You didn't find anything about the case Fritz was on."

Gojon gave me a single negative shake of his head, the shadow shifting sidewise this time. "And several pages were missing from his desk calendar.'' He spoke thoughtfully, but the thoughts were not new ones.

"No messages on his answering machine?"

"If there were any, the thief wiped them."

"All right, Commissaire," I said tightly, "your turn. How did it happen? Your message skipped most of the details."

"Monsieur Donhoff was on foot in the Rue de la Montagne Sainte Geneviève when he was shot," Gojon said in a quiet, measured tone. "Less than a block above Place Maubert. Now, that is only a ten-minute walk from his apartment. But there was a cold rain that night, verging on sleet. So it does not seem likely he'd merely gone out for an aimless stroll."

"Not likely," I agreed.

"But none of the neighborhood people we've questioned so far appears to know any reason for his being there." Gojon was silent for a moment, and then continued with the details in his habitual stiff manner.

"The bullets taken out of Monsieur Donhoff are .38 caliber. Nobody seems to have seen the shooting. But quite a number in nearby apartments heard the shots. When they looked out their windows, they saw a man crouching over Monsieur Donhoff's fallen figure, hastily removing things from his pockets. We've put together all the descriptions of this man," Gojon added drily. "He was a tall short man, thin and stocky, bareheaded with a black cap, wearing a raincoat or short leather jacket. The usual. No help at all."

"He must have seen Fritz was still alive," I said. "But he didn't shoot him again."

"That may be just luck. A patrol car happened to be cruising across Place Maubert at the time. The two cops in it heard the shots and backed up and drove in as fast as they could. When their car turned into the street the man crouched over Monsieur Donhoff straightened up and fired four shots at it. Then he ran away, up the street."

"Four at the patrol car," I said, "and two into Fritz. A

six-shot revolver. No bullets left and no time for him to finish off Fritz a slower way.''

Sometimes the cops *are* around when you need them.

''Some of those last shots smashed the car's windshield,'' Gojon told me. ''The driver ducked and lost control. Swerved into the metal post of a streetlamp. By the time the two cops climbed out the shooter was around the corner, into Rue des Écoles. They ran after him, but he'd already jumped into a waiting car. A dark sedan—Citroën, probably. It disappeared before they could get its license.''

''And you haven't come up with anything else.''

''Not so far,'' Gojon acknowledged. ''Shall I drop you off at your apartment?''

''I'd like to see where it happened first.''

Gojon drove across the Seine to the Left Bank, taking Rue Saint Jacques and turning left on Boulevard Saint Germain. There was no traffic at all at that time of the morning. And Fritz had been taken to the hospital nearest to the place where he'd been shot. We made it in less than six minutes.

As Victor Hugo noted, you can get vertigo looking too deeply into the past horrors associated with almost any corner of old Paris.

Place Maubert, surrounded by its food markets, office buildings, and residential blocks, is a peaceful enough spot these days. By night it settles into a safe and quiet sleep. Not like it used to be, back in the Middle Ages.

Place Maubert by night, back then, was a dark, dangerous inferno. A favorite roistering center for violent gangs of thugs and impoverished, hell-bent students. Along with rock-bottom whores and women of a more deadly disposition— like the trio of professional poisoners who wound up being killed by the fumes of a new batch they were cooking up.

By day, in the vain hope of discouraging such sinners, the government used Place Maubert for executions. A favorite long-running show for crowds seeking a little diversion. Villon, a good poet and bad character who was both thug and student, narrowly escaped the gibbet permanently set up there. Hanging was the simplest method of execution. Other prisoners were first hung and then burned. They were the lucky ones. When the government really disliked someone it skipped the hanging part. He or she was burned while still alive.

There's a bronze statue there now of one of the unlucky. Étienne Dolet, a printer-publisher condemned for blasphemy four hundred years ago. No need to spend money on costly firewood in his case. They piled all his books around him and set them ablaze. The audience loved it.

Commissaire Gojon drove us past the unfortunate Dolet's statue and turned into one of the nine streets leading out of Place Maubert. A narrow, steeply climbing street: Rue de la Montagne Sainte Geneviève. He parked next to a lamppost that had been bent to the pavement, its light smashed. "Here is where the patrol car crashed."

He climbed out of the car. I followed him up the sidewalk. He stopped and said, "This is where Monsieur Donhoff fell."

I glanced around. There was a dark, recessed doorway nearby. "Was he standing here or walking past when he was shot?"

"We don't know that," Gojon said. "Does he have any friends close by that he might have been visiting?"

"Not that I know of," I told him. "Made *any* progress checking the people who live around here?"

"We haven't turned up any that say they know Monsieur Donhoff—as yet. But our investigation has barely begun."

I looked up toward the top of the street. It wasn't far. The "mountain" of its name is less than two hundred feet high. Just a hill that became the main Roman residential district after Julius Caesar's troops conquered the native Parisi tribe and settled in.

That was fifty years before Christ was born. Three centuries later the Roman settlement was wiped out by invading barbarian hordes. And a couple centuries after that Geneviève became the patron saint of Paris when her prayers turned away another horde, led by Attila the Hun. For a long time her remains were kept in a crypt at the top of this street. Until the Revolution's wave of antireligious fervor. Then Sainte Geneviève's remains were dumped into the river. But the revolutionary fervor came and went, and she is again Paris's patron saint. With the hill named after her and the street named after the hill.

There's little visible now to remind you of any of that long history of ups and downs. Few of the apartment houses lining the steep, narrow street are more than a couple centuries old. Most of the ground-floor spaces are small shops and restaurants. Between them covered passages lead into interior courtyards enclosed by more apartment buildings.

The police had their work cut out for them, checking on everyone in these blocks.

I saw nothing that gave me a clue to what Fritz might have been up to there on a cold rainy night.

As we walked back down to Gojon's car I said, "If you dig up something useful, I'll appreciate your letting me know about it."

"I was about to tell you the same," Gojon said. "I assume you're going to do some digging on your own. And you don't have my handicap—a dozen other important cases requiring my full attention. I *expect* you to inform me of whatever you find out."

I said, "Sure."

Gojon turned his head and gave me a long, hard look. "I know what Fritz Donhoff means to you, Sawyer. That *won't* serve as an excuse if you take justice into your own hands."

Crow had warned me, before I headed for the airport, "Do something about that expression and tone of voice, Pete. Especially around any cops that know half as much about you as I do. You're advertising what you want to do to whoever shot Fritz."

But my head had been too full of the way Fritz looked right now for me to concentrate on acting. And Commissaire Gojon did know me.

"The law handles justice in this country," he added in that subdued tone that meant he wasn't kidding around. "So anything you learn you just turn over to me. Promptly."

I said, "Sure," again. This time with what I hoped sounded like more sincerity.

Gojon dropped me off outside the fenced courtyard inside which I kept an apartment adjacent to Fritz's, for whenever work or pleasure brought me up to Paris. I waited until his car was gone. Then I walked half a block to Place Contrescarpe.

The Café Les Arts had closed for the night. But there was still some late clientele inside the glass-enclosed terraces of two other bistros: La Chope and the Contrescarpe Bar. I scanned both as I crossed the *place*. Nobody unusual in them. I went two more blocks to the garage where I kept my Paris car.

It was a Renault 5. There was a hidden compartment inside the backseat. The pistol in it was a compact model Beretta with fourteen rounds in its magazine. My car gun used to be a Mauser, until I'd had to use it in circumstances that made ditching it essential. There was a twin of this Beretta concealed in my apartment. But what had happened to Fritz suggested it might not be advisable to go in there unarmed.

I jacked the first round into the chamber and made sure the safety was on before tucking the gun into my belt under my jacket. Then I walked back across the *place* to my address.

Several old restored houses were grouped around the small courtyard hidden from the street by the fence. My apartment and Fritz's were next to each other on the second floor of one house. I glanced up at our adjacent living-room windows as I crossed the uneven cobbles, past the bare-branched tree in the middle of the courtyard. Both windows were as they should be—dark.

The buzzer button by the door below them unlocked the house door and snapped on the interior stairway light for twenty seconds. I took out my key ring as I went up the stairs to the landing between our apartment doors. One of the keys was to Fritz's place. And he had one to mine, which meant that whoever had taken his key ring had it now. Question: Which to check first—Fritz's apartment, to see if the cops and the robbers had missed something, or my own to see if that had been tossed, too.

I was deciding to look in mine first when I heard a noise inside Fritz's apartment.

4

IT WASN'T MUCH OF A NOISE. SOMETHING LIKE A BOOK BE-ing dropped on the floor inside.

I made a fast shift of the keys to my left hand, got the Beretta out of my belt, and thumbed off its safety.

There was another small noise on the other side of Fritz's closed door, similar to the first.

I poised my key close to my own door lock and waited a couple more seconds. The stairway light snapped off. I went into my living room with the best combination of speed and quietness I could manage, dodging to my left inside, ready to shoot at anyone waiting for me in there.

Nobody was. I went swiftly through the living room, down the corridor past my kitchen and bathroom, into the back bedroom. Still nobody. Stepping into my clothes closet there, I crouched low and worked a hidden lock. That opened a secret door that looked like it was just part of the wallpapered back wall of the closet. I went through it into Fritz's clothes closet.

Our apartments were laid out identically. His closet door was open, showing me his dark bedroom. Staying crouched, I moved silently through it and along his corridor. A faint light was showing at the other end, inside the living room. I crouched lower when I neared that end and eased myself forward, making no sound at all. I stopped when I saw his shadowy figure outlined against the living-room window.

He appeared to be about my height and bulky. The beam of the small flashlight he held was aimed at the inside of the apartment door. So was the revolver in his other hand. Aiming my Beretta at the middle of his bulky torso, I straightened, took a long step into the living room, and hit the wall light switch with my left hand.

His reaction to the sudden blaze of light was instant. Before I could warn him to freeze he was twisting around with that revolver. He had a problem, though. He didn't know exactly where I was. In the split second before he could find out I shot him.

A 9mm Beretta doesn't make as big a bang as a .45. But it sounded big enough in the confines of the room. The bullet broke his right arm, close to the elbow, and spun him against Fritz's desk. His gun and flashlight spilled out of his hands, bounced off the desktop, and fell out of sight behind it. He fell in the opposite direction and landed in the middle of the living-room floor with a heavy thump and a soft grunt.

He sat up quickly, grabbing his wrecked arm with his left hand. There was some dull shock in his expression, but that was all. The pain hadn't hit him yet.

He had a meaty face without much forehead. His bulk included a broad, solid belly. He stared at me with eyes that no variety of nastiness could surprise, and that wouldn't register anything that wasn't nasty.

"What did you come back here for?" I asked him. "Forget something?"

He only gritted his teeth and narrowed those eyes. The pain was coming through now.

"Or wasn't it you who hit this place before?"

I don't know if he was giving any thought to answering that. If he was, it was interrupted by a light knocking at Fritz's apartment door.

A woman's voice called through it softly. "Monsieur Donhoff? It's me, Yvette . . . I'm sorry I'm so late, but you did say to come *whenever* I got back to Paris. And I saw your light on . . .''

The guy sitting on the floor looked at the door with something changing in his expression. I couldn't tell what the change meant. But the voice wasn't familiar to me, and though Fritz did have a lot of lady friends, he hadn't gotten around to telling me about any new one named Yvette. I moved over against the wall near the door. On the side of it where its knob and inside lock were.

"Monsieur Donhoff . . . ?'' She sounded worried now. "Are you all right? I heard something . . .''

Keeping myself against the wall, I reached out carefully with my left hand to unlock the door. My right hand held the Beretta ready to deal with anything unpleasant that came through.

The door slammed wide open before I could touch it. The guy sitting on the floor hadn't relocked it from inside.

What came through was too fast for me. There were two identical sounds out on the staircase landing. Neither was louder than a discreet cough.

The torso of the guy sitting on the floor went over backward. His head bounced once on the floor. After that he didn't move again. They usually don't, with a bullet in the heart and another in the brain.

I dropped to one knee, hugging the wall. Hearing someone running away down the stairs didn't hearten me too much. She could have a partner with her. One of them running away and the other waiting on the landing for me to act foolish.

But I couldn't continue to huddle against the wall forever. Shoving off my knee, I did a low dive past the open doorway, turned to shoot anybody out there. The landing was empty. I hit the floor on my shoulder and came up on my feet looking down through the living-room window at the dark courtyard.

The door between the courtyard and the street was like the

one to the house. You had to press a buzzer button on one side or the other to unlock it. At the same time it turned on the courtyard lamp for a short period. She hadn't gone out that way yet. I opened the window and aimed the Beretta down through it, waiting.

A full minute went by. Nothing happened. I cursed, went out of the apartment, and ran down the stairs. At the bottom I found what I'd thought I'd find. She had gone out the *back* door, leaving it open. Behind the house was a passageway leading to a different street. From that point on there were too many little streets, alleys, and passages for me to waste time trying to find her. I wouldn't recognize her, anyway, unless she was helpful enough to be walking around still carrying the murder weapon in her hand.

I trudged back up the stairs to Fritz's apartment, shut the door, and turned the inside lock. Then I put my Beretta down on the desk and phoned Commissaire Gojon's home number.

His voice came through sounding a little groggy. When he heard who it was the voice got irritated as well. "For God's sake, Sawyer, I was just getting back into bed."

"You told me to be prompt, if I found anything."

"You mean you have, already?" Gojon snapped it, but the groggy anger was gone.

I told him what I had found.

"Did you call the police yet?"

"I was under the impression I was talking to them now."

"I mean . . ."

"I know what you mean. No, I didn't. But if somebody else around here heard the shot I fired they may have phoned for the police. I don't want to have to answer a lot of questions that you already know the answers to."

"I'm on my way," Gojon said, and hung up.

I put down the phone, crouched over the dead man on the floor, and went through his pockets. According to his ID his name was Paul Dupuy. The only other items of interest on him were two key rings. One was Fritz's, with the New York City Police medallion he'd been given as a souvenir on a visit to the States.

Putting everything back in Paul Dupuy's pockets, I went around the desk and took a close look at his revolver, not touching it. Sure enough: it was a .38. A six-shot Colt Detective Special with the two-inch barrel. A long way from its native America, where it challenged the five-shot Smith & Wesson Chiefs Special as the FBI's favorite snub-nosed weapon.

I'd have been willing to bet some heavy money that this one would prove to be the gun that put the two slugs into Fritz. If I was right, that plus Fritz's key ring would peg the late Paul Dupuy as the one who had shot Fritz and searched his apartment.

Then why would he have come back there tonight?

One simple explanation. He was there waiting for me. Set to shoot me when I walked in the door. With the woman farther up the stairway waiting to come down, box me in, and make sure of the kill.

But they hadn't been able to nail me, and she had killed Dupuy instead. Why? Another simple explanation: So he wouldn't be able to talk.

Too simple.

Less simple explanation: The dead man on the floor had unwittingly been the real target of the setup. I could come up with one possible motive for that, but it was riddled with ifs and maybes. So I let it drop and looked at my Beretta on the desk. I decided to leave it there, in plain sight. Indicating to the cops that I wasn't worried about it.

My story would be that the Beretta had been in my place, and I'd picked it up before coming into Fritz's. People have a right in France to keep a gun at home "for protection of domicile." What I didn't have a right to do was to walk around outside with a deadly weapon. A private investigator can't get a permanent carry permit in France.

According to the rules you can only get a short-term carry permit. For that you have to make an application explaining why it's required for a specific situation. It takes a lot of time and red tape. The rules weren't written to help you survive sudden emergencies. Which is why I've broken them now and then. As cautiously as circumstances allowed.

I expected to break them again soon. Because I had more than a premonition that I hadn't had my last encounter with the spooky woman responsible for the corpse on the floor. I didn't know who she was or what she looked like or how she was involved in whatever was going on. But one thing about her I did know. She could shoot fast enough and straight enough to give Annie Oakley a hard time.

5

I LEFT CALLING ON MIMI NOGARET UNTIL SEVEN O'CLOCK the following evening. Mimi could unleash a vicious temper if you disturbed her before she fixed her hair, did her make-up, and had her breakfast.

My day was a full one before I got around to her. At eight in the morning I was back in the hospital to check on Fritz's condition. He was still unconscious. The surgeon in charge of his case said his vital signs were encouraging.

"Then why doesn't he wake up?"

The doctor started to give me some standard medical gibberish, then took a good look at my face and changed his mind. "I don't really know, to be honest. Perhaps Monsieur Donhoff is conserving himself. I've known some patients to use up the last of their strength fighting to come to, and then dying. Perhaps his nervous system knows best, and is using the coma to build his strength."

"Perhaps," I repeated bleakly.

The doctor nodded. "I'm afraid I can't be more definite than that at this point."

I spent an hour at Fritz's bedside. That didn't accomplish anything except to tighten the pressure inside me. Finally I phoned Commissaire Gojon's office. He had some facts by then.

Ballistics had confirmed it: the .38 revolver carried by Paul

Dupuy had fired the bullets removed from Fritz. In my opinion that wasn't proof positive that Dupuy was the one who'd fired those two bullets. But one thing I *was* sure of: the mysterious woman who'd killed Dupuy hadn't shot Fritz. If she had, Fritz would have died on the spot.

The police hadn't turned up any more about her than I'd told them. But they had a fat dossier on Paul Dupuy.

He'd been an enforcer-collector for several heavy-money loan sharks. Over the years the cops had lodged a number of charges against him. Four times for assaulting debtors late with their interest payments, twice for murdering ones who'd given up trying to pay. A skillful lawyer and reluctant witnesses had combined to force the law to drop the charges each time.

"But we start digging deeper into that background today," Gojon told me. "We'll be questioning all his known *milieu* contacts, as well as those specifically involved in loan-sharking. I'll let you know when we come up with something."

I doubted that he would. I had a feeling Paul Dupuy had been killed for the express purpose of diverting any investigation to his background—instead of in some other direction that *was* connected with the shooting of Fritz Donhoff. But I didn't tell Gojon that. First of all because I could be wrong. The case Fritz had been on *might* be somehow involved with loan-sharking. And Gojon had the manpower needed to check that out thoroughly.

So I left him searching for leads in that direction while I went off hunting in another.

Actually, I didn't have a specific alternate direction. Just a diversity of people, some on the shady side of the law, that I knew Fritz sometimes consulted when he was after information. I spent the rest of that day prowling around Paris, trying to discover if he had contacted any of them this time.

None of them had anything to tell me—until I got to Mimi Nogaret's house, tucked away behind a tiny walled garden in a short, stylish block between the Arc de Triomphe and the Seine.

Mimi had become habituated to being wide awake all night and sleeping through the day during her years of professional life. But she had finished her breakfast and was pouring herself her ritual third cup of coffee when her maid, Mademoiselle Corinne, ushered me into her boudoir at seven P.M.

Two lamps with orange shades enveloped Mimi in a soft, warm glow. Wearing a white satin dressing gown trimmed with lace, she sat in a scarlet plush chaise longue with a black wicker bedtray across her slim lap. Her gilded hair and extensive makeup were just so. She greeted me with a fond smile.

"Pierre-Ange, you never grow older. You still look like a boy—delicious enough to bite into, even with a full set of dentures."

Which didn't mean much except that she'd had decades of practice at welcoming men in that fashion. I bent and kissed both of her ravaged cheeks.

Mimi probed my midsection with experienced fingers. "And still firm as a flat rock. My girls would have enjoyed you."

There was a photograph of Mimi on the mantel behind her, taken when she was a handsome thirty. She was now about eighty. The similarities between the photographed face and the real woman made the differences unnerving. Like looking at a picture of the Acropolis when it was the glory of classical Greece and at the same time seeing the ruin the devouring centuries had made of it.

She pointed to the coffeepot and told her maid, "Refill this, and bring another coffee service for Monsieur Sawyer." Mimi gave the order slowly and distinctly, as though speaking to a child who hadn't quite learned the rudiments of her job. Mademoiselle Corinne was, after all, only sixty, and hadn't been in Mimi Nogaret's employ more than forty-two years.

When her maid left with the pot, Mimi gestured for me to sit down. The chair was by a window, shuttered now, that overlooked her little walled-in garden. The garden, like everything about the four-story house, was as well kept as it had been in 1946. That was the year Mimi Nogaret's house had ceased to be a paying proposition. When the new French law closed all the legal brothels.

Before that it had been one of the most famous establishments in Paris. With a stable of high-priced prostitutes and a prosperous clientele devoted to the ingenious variety of its pleasure rooms. There was one that looked like a pirate captain's cabin, another like the luxurious harem tent of a desert sheik, and one like an Oriental emperor's bedroom-cum-torture chamber. Almost any kink a man could afford had its own room at Mimi's place, with appropriate costumes to heighten the fantasy.

She had never herself been a whore—Mimi made certain everyone understood that. She had just owned and managed the establishment. "Merely a businesswoman, dealing in a legal commodity and turning an honest franc." She had turned enough francs, by the time her place was closed down, to keep all the special rooms exactly as they'd been in the heyday of her house. It was her dream that after her death the government would take it over as a museum of a cherished and lost way of life.

"Why not?" Mimi demanded of the dubious. "It is as much a part of French history now as the Versailles."

"I guess you've heard about what happened to Fritz on Saturday night," I said. I was sure she would have by now, though she seldom paid attention to the news media and never left the house. Many of her former clients dropped in to visit her regularly, out of nostalgia, bringing her gossip—including some secret goings-on—of the outside world.

"Yes," she told me with a small frown, "I heard. If he's dead please don't tell me. I don't want to know it. So many old friends go away lately . . ."

"He's not dead. He's putting up a fight. And he does have the basic health to fight with."

Mimi nodded, her smile as small as her frown. "He certainly did look as fit as ever when I saw him last."

"When was that?" I asked her.

"He visited me Friday night."

I sat up straighter. "What did he come to see you about?"

"People don't always come here *wanting* something from me," she said with a slight pout. "I *am* amusing to simply visit with, though you may be too young to appreciate that."

"What did Fritz come about?" I repeated.

Mimi responded to my tone by dropping the banter. "He wanted to know if I've heard anything recent about Arnaud Galice."

The father of Arnaud Galice had been in the Paris Resistance with Fritz, and had made a career in French Intelligence for several decades after the war. The son, after failing at careers in journalism and then advertising, had begun using his father's connections to deal in free-lance espionage. Both the commercial and political varieties. Selling information to whoever would pay the most for it.

Fritz and I had gotten involved after an industrialist hired us to find out why his company's secrets were leaking to his competitors. The trail led to Arnaud Galice. He had been seducing the information out of a high-placed company secretary.

He didn't look the part of a seducer of women, I remembered from the two times we'd met. A portly man of medium height, with short, heavy legs. In his midthirties and prematurely bald, with chunky features. The expression of his eyes came back to me most strongly—they'd held a permanent greedy glitter.

But a jaunty grin, brimming with self-confidence, makes up for a lot of other flaws. Coupled with his impeccable taste in expensive tailored clothes. That particular secretary was not the first to fall for Arnaud Galice.

His father had been a sick man by then, with less than a year to live. Out of compassion for him, Fritz had tipped off the son before we turned over our findings and the law went after him. They didn't find him. But rumors had come our way, for a time, of Arnaud Galice working other rackets in distant parts of the world under other names.

"I thought somebody caught up with Galice a couple years ago," I told Mimi. "Somebody who killed him. In Instanbul."

"I heard the same," Mimi said. "But Fritz said it might not be true. He thought he might have seen him, here in Paris."

"*Might* have?"

"Yes." Mimi thought about it. "Fritz didn't sound *sure* of it."

"Where did he think he saw him? In what connection?"

"I don't know, Pierre-Ange. Fritz didn't say and I didn't ask. He just wanted to know if any rumor about Galice being around lately had come my way. When I said no, he asked me to put out feelers among my friends."

A number of Mimi's friends had been—like Fritz—part of wartime Resistance groups. Her brothel had been a favorite of Nazi officers and Vichy officials. Mimi and her girls were good at unobtrusive eavesdropping. She passed on useful items to her Resistance contacts. Some of those contacts were currently senior members of the Intelligence establishment, while others kept in touch with its old-boy network.

"Have any of *them* come across anything recent about Galice?" I asked her.

"None I've spoken to so far. But I will keep asking. And those I've already asked will let me know if they learn anything."

"And you'll let *me* know?"

Mimi tilted her head and eyed me through lowered lashes. The smile she gave me this time cut three decades off the five between her and that photograph of her.

''I never could resist a beautiful man,'' she said in a low, husky voice.

I smiled back at her like a delighted idiot, though if Mimi Nogaret had ever in her life had a romantic attachment to any man it would be news to everyone who'd known her.

Mademoiselle Corinne came back into the boudoir before this romance could shrivel into disillusion.

6

THERE WAS A CHANGE AT THE HÔTEL DIEU. COMMISSAIRE Gojon now had two men guarding Fritz's room. My account of the efficiency with which the unknown woman had knocked off Paul Dupuy had impressed him. Enough to agree that a single guard might not discourage her if she wanted to get at Fritz.

What hadn't changed was Fritz's condition.

I drove home from the hospital to check his answering machine and my own. There was no pertinent message on either. I phoned two Intelligence contacts of my own. Both knew of Arnaud Galice's past. Neither had any reason to think he might still be alive and operating once more in Paris. They said they would make inquiries, here and with Istanbul.

Next I called Gojon. He told me police interrogation of Paul Dupuy's underworld connections hadn't so far turned up anything connecting him to Fritz or any female assassin. I told him about Arnaud Galice. Gojon had never heard the name before. I asked him to have the police try it on everyone questioned in the future, both among the *milieu* and around Place Maubert. The more people out there asking about Galice, the better my chance of getting a clue to Fritz's sudden interest in him.

My last call was to the Paris apartment of Jean-Marie Reju. He was one of the best and most highly priced personal bodyguards in Europe, having established his reputation working in that capacity for the French government before going private. A taciturn, difficult character, Reju allowed himself very few friends. Over the past couple years he'd come to regard me as one of those few.

One reason for Reju's deserved reputation was that he kept himself informed about any new potential sources of assassination or kidnap attempts. Which meant that he might know of some woman who could handle a gun with the swift sureness of the one who had done the job on Paul Dupuy. Also, Reju just might have heard something current about Arnaud Galice.

Reju wasn't home. The phone there was answered by the man who had shared the big apartment with him for the last ten years. Gregory Petrov. He was a count, a title that would have meant a good deal more if Russia were still run by a tsar. In the real world Petrov was a cultivated, good-natured, and exquisitely polite businessman with a prosperous jewelry shop on the Champs-Élysées.

He asked after my health, was genuinely upset to learn about Fritz, and told me that Jean-Marie Reju was away convoying a Swedish multimillionaire on a business trip through Europe. "I really don't know which city they are in tonight," Petrov said. "But Jean-Marie sometimes phones me to see if he's had any professional calls."

I asked him to tell Reju to phone me when he called next time. Gregory Petrov said he would. I went out to Place Contrescarpe and had a Lebanese dinner.

The Liban Restaurant has photos of the owner's native land on the brick walls, hung there out of nostalgia for the beauty that rival Mideast political and religious thugs have chopped into oatmeal. I was in Beirut once before Lebanon's twenty-sided civil war had gotten really bad, and once again after it was well advanced, looking for a kid reporter who had disappeared. I won't say I couldn't recognize the place the second time. It was worse than that: I did recognize it—

like recognizing parts of somebody who has been in a ninety-mile-per-hour car crash.

It was the scariest city I've ever been in, outside of Belfast and parts of Chicago on a Saturday night.

But Beirut had had good restaurants, and the Liban on Contrescarpe rivaled the best. I had the *kebbe boulettes* and *foie de volailles* with *foul*, *homos*, and *laban concombre*, and returned to my apartment savoring their combined taste.

There was nothing new on my answering machine. I went next door and checked Fritz's.

That one did have a new message on it. I played it twice.

It was a woman's voice. Unmistakably American. Just as unmistakably *not* the voice of the woman who'd fired the two silenced shots through Fritz's doorway last night.

"Monsieur Donhoff, this is Susan Kape. I expected to have heard something from you by now. Have you found out anything yet? And were you able to make contact with your partner? Remember, he has to be in Rome by tomorrow evening. If he can't, we have to arrange for someone else professional to be there. Please, do call me back before *too* late tonight."

I didn't know Susan Kape's phone number and I didn't waste time trying to find it. Leaving the house, I got back into my Renault and drove across the Pont de Sully to the other side of the Seine. I didn't need to make any inquiries about who the name Susan Kape belonged to or where I'd be likely to find her.

7

THE MANSIONS BUILT BY THE GRAND OLD FAMILIES AND THE new rich in the Marais quarter made it the most fashionable in Paris during the first half of the eighteenth century. The best location was in the section surrounding the Place des Vosges, notorious for the number of noblemen wounded and killed in it before the neighborhood became so richly residential and dueling was outlawed there. The big square, with its stone arcades and chestnut and elm trees, was called the Place Royale in those days.

But by the nineteenth century the new-money favorite was the Faubourg St. Honoré, and the old money had moved over to the Faubourg St. Germain. The Marais went downhill. Some of the big mansions were abandoned, others became factories or warehouses, the rest were cut up into little dirt-cheap rooms for rent. By the Second World War it was close to becoming a slum.

Then, a couple decades ago, Paris decided to try a shot of urban renewal on the neighborhood. Not the way cities usually go about it: demolishing perfectly solid dwellings and replacing them with bleak, fragile high-rises. Instead they began shining up the old buildings and converting their high-ceilinged interiors into spacious apartments. The area around the Place des Vosges is once more in vogue, among those who can afford the better things of life.

I parked less than two blocks from the *place*, outside a late-seventeenth-century townhouse majestically constructed around three sides of a large flagstone courtyard facing the street. Susan Kape didn't own an apartment in this restored mansion. All of it was hers. Anybody who occasionally checked the currents up in the social stratosphere knew that—and many other things about Susan Kape's life. Susan Kape was one of the wealthiest young women in the world.

The building had become a plumbing supplies factory, with the courtyard used for parking its delivery trucks, before her father bought it. Simon Kape redid it to serve as European headquarters for his Texas-based oil and chemicals company. After his death Susan Kape shifted the company offices down to the tax haven of Monaco and made this place her home.

The entrance to its main building and two wings was inside the courtyard, and the wrought-iron courtyard gate was locked. I pressed a button next to it. Presumably it rang a bell somewhere inside, but the walls in there were much too thick for the sound to reach me.

After a while the courtyard lamps went on. Just before they did I spotted a figure standing on the edge of the right-wing roof, looking down in my direction. When the courtyard lit up I saw the figure held something long and shiny. A marksman's rifle, almost certainly, with a night scope.

I waited. A door in the left wing opened. A man emerged and came toward the inside of the gate.

Average height, sturdy build, about thirty years old. Wearing tight designer jeans tucked into short boots and a black shirt with a gleam like silk. He'd hung a leather jacket over his shoulders against the cold outside. The leather was thin and supple, the kind that costs a mint.

When he got close I recognized him. I'd seen him a couple times before. In Monaco, with Susan Kape. He'd seemed to be working as her combination driver and bodyguard.

"Yes?" he demanded, studying me through the locked gate. Not unfriendly; just guarded. He didn't know me.

He was a good-looking guy, with black curly hair and neatly chiseled features. Breton ancestry, probably. He had that dark Celtic look of country people along that rugged part of the Atlantic coast of France. That introverted stubbornness, so often containing a streak of moody mysticism.

"I want to see Susan Kape," I told him. "My name is Pierre-Ange Sawyer."

He wasn't slow. "Monsieur Donhoff's partner?" I nodded, and he asked me for some ID. I handed my wallet through the gate's bars. He opened it, glanced at the photograph on my *carte de travail*, and stopped looking wary. Handing back my wallet, he took a key from his pocket.

"This is a surprise," he said as he unlocked the gate. "We thought you were down on the Côte d'Azur. Or maybe on your way to Rome." He had what used to be called a working-class accent, before workers got upwardly mobile and categorizing people that way became déclassé.

He relocked the gate behind me before leading the way across the courtyard. I pointed to the figure on the roof. "Got many more like that around here?"

"Three altogether."

"Round the clock?"

"Sure. Each team handles an eight-hour shift."

Nine expert marksmen on guard duty through each twenty-four hours don't come cheap. But the Kape company probably spent more on paper clips.

We entered a brightly lighted hallway in the left wing. "You mind waiting here?" he said, waving a muscular, short-fingered left hand at a couple wing chairs. The hand had an unusual number of small, long-healed scars. "She'll want to meet you, but right now she's busy with Monsieur Petulla. He's head of her firm's legal staff."

That would make this Petulla one of the small team of business specialists who managed Susan Kape's company interests for her. The same team her father had used, but with a difference. Simon Kape had directed every move any member of his team made. Under the daughter, the team made the decisions and explained them to her at regular intervals. An arrangement that seemed to work. It was a very healthy company, according to the financial pages of the *International Herald Tribune*.

I said I didn't mind waiting. "You know my name," I added, "but I don't know yours."

"Sorry. Sometimes I forget to introduce myself." He said it drily, perhaps with a slightly bitter twist. "I'm Yann Bouvier." He held out his hand, and I noticed this one also had a lot of old scars.

His name registered while we shook hands. "You're the one who rescued her in the mountains."

"I didn't *rescue* her," he said. "All I did was stay with her till the rescue team got there."

It had been about two and a half years ago. Susan Kape and two other society thrill-seekers had decided to go over the Alps in a hot air balloon. Their gondola struck a peak, killing the other two. She was dumped over a cliff and landed on a ledge, smashing both hips and legs.

Yann Bouvier had been a rock-climbing enthusiast who made his living as a mason. Both the job and the hobby explained the scars. He'd been on holiday, making a solitary climb near where the balloon crashed, and was the only one who saw where Susan Kape fell. He managed to climb down to her but then couldn't get back up. So he stayed with her, shouting for help every half hour. It took one of the rescue teams two days to find them and get them off the ledge. When she could speak, some days later, she'd said she wouldn't have lived through it if it hadn't been for Yann Bouvier.

I said, "A couple months ago some of the gossip columnists were predicting the two of you were going to get married."

"We were talking about it," he acknowledged somewhat

defensively. "Who knows, we still might. No rush." He
seemed to be searching my expression for a smirk. I didn't
give him any. It didn't bother me if he'd parlayed the rescue
into a cushy life—and the prospect of an even cushier marriage. It seemed to bother him, though.

He turned away from me and went off along the hallway
to my right, disappearing around a corner there. I took off
my topcoat, tucked my cap into one of its pockets and my
wool scarf into the other, and draped it across one of the
chairs. I didn't feel like sitting down while I waited. The
primitive hunting instinct pushes at you to get familiar with
new terrain as quickly as possible. Before the tigers that have
been prowling that territory all their lives catch your scent.

The hallway was unnaturally bright because the walls, and
the ceiling fourteen feet above my head, had recently been
repainted. Off-white. And nothing had been installed yet,
other than the two chairs, to absorb the reflections. No other
furniture, no pictures on the walls, no rugs on the newly
polished floor. I sauntered through an open door into a room
to my left.

It turned out to be two very large rooms, connected by a
wide archway. The paint job there was just as new, and the
lighting just as bright. The only furniture in both rooms con-
sisted of long, narrow tables. Most were against the walls,
with some others grouped in the middle of each room. Half
the tables were empty. The rest held assorted treasures of
antiquity.

The centerpiece on the table nearest to me was a silver
statuette, about one foot tall, of a graceful nude braiding
seashells into her long hair. The card underneath identified
it as a Venus Anadyomene of the second century A.D., unearthed in Carthage in 1932.

The other objects on the table were large gold and silver
platters and flasks, each decorated with mythological scenes
and all, like the Venus statuette, from various points around
the outskirts of the Roman Empire.

Simon Kape's hobby had been collecting ancient decorative and fine arts. Not a hobby for the merely middling rich, when pursued to this extent. My mother, Babette, was an art historian, and I hadn't been able to avoid having some of the basics drubbed into me. I'd had cases since, involving art theft and forgery, that taught me more. By my rough estimate the items on that one table alone would bring well over a million dollars in the current world of high-pressure art auctions. And some of the other tables in that room held treasures of equal value: Roman, Greek, Egyptian, Etruscan . . .

About seven months ago Susan Kape had announced her intention of turning most of her Paris mansion into a museum bearing her father's name. Using his collection as a start and gradually adding to it. Unlike Mimi Nogaret, she didn't have to put her faith in government support to fulfill her dream. The company Susan Kape had inherited was committed to funding the museum forever. Which betrayed a touching faith of her own, in the longevity of the capitalist system.

I hoped, for her sake, that the place acquired, sooner rather than later, a better antiburglary system than I'd seen evidence of so far. An experienced gang could tunnel up through the floor and take out the choicest items while the three marksmen on guard duty were prowling other approaches to the mansion.

I walked through the wide archway into the second room. There, too, half the display tables were still empty. The others held decorated pottery and copper, stone and terra-cotta sculptures from pre-Colombian Central America.

As in the first room, this one had four video cameras maintaining surveillance from the ceiling corners. An easy system for experts to render useless. I was about to crouch down and look for electronic devices under the tables when a young woman came in through a door on the other side of the room.

She was small and slender in a loose-fitting denim shirt, aging dungarees, and scuffed saddle shoes, with extra-large horn-rimmed glasses perched on the flattish bridge of her small nose. Her crisp gingery-red hair made a startling mismatch with her Oriental features. She was carrying what looked like an Olmec jaguar mask carved out of basalt.

"You must be Monsieur Donhoff's partner," she said with a hesitant smile. "Yann just told me you were here."

I nodded and watched her place the basalt mask carefully on a table between two jade figurines: chimeras, part animal and part human. She put an identification card down beside the mask before turning back to me.

"I'm Carmen Haung," she told me, and shook my hand. Maybe she saw the name didn't register, because she added, "Susan's antiquities adviser."

"Does that make you the curator here?"

"This isn't a museum yet. It has a long way to go before anyone needs to be given official titles." Her French was rougher than Susan Kape's. Carmen Haung had the vocabulary but kept hesitating over how to put it together correctly. "So far my job has been mainly cataloging her father's collection, so we can see where the biggest gaps are that need filling."

I switched to English. "What part of the States are you from?"

She looked relieved to shift languages. "Hawaii, can't you guess?" She gestured at her face and hair.

"Chinese—" I hazarded, "—and what, Scottish?"

"You're not a bad detective. Add a large dollop of Portuguese and you've got me."

"Exotic."

Carmen Haung made a rueful face. "Exotic—that's a polite way of saying weird."

"It's a way of saying fascinating."

"Oh?" She took off her glasses. Dangled them in her hand and studied me anew. Without the glasses she had to narrow her slanty eyes to see me clearly. "Your *name* is kind of exotic," she said after a moment. "Pierre-Ange—if you translate that literally into English it comes out Stone Angel."

"I know."

"You don't look much like an angel."

"I'm still working on that."

"More like a devil, actually. Sort of a nice one, though." Her smile was still tentative. Flirting was a sport she hadn't practiced much. "I suppose we'll be flying to Rome together, now that you're here. Instead of having to meet up there as originally planned."

"Why are we going to Rome?"

She looked puzzled. "Didn't Monsieur Donhoff explain that to you?"

I told her why Fritz had been unable to explain anything to me.

Carmen Haung stared at me, shocked. "But . . . that's awful. . . . What . . ." She fumbled with the question she wanted to ask.

Her shock seemed genuine to me. You get practice at reading people in my business. Even so, you can be wrong. So can a pro poker player. I didn't think I was wrong this time. Carmen Haung wasn't faking it. Fritz getting shot was news to her.

That wouldn't be too strange. It had happened late Saturday night. The regular Paris papers don't come out on Sunday. By Monday, today, it was last week's news. And the wounding during a robbery of a man whose name didn't mean anything to the general public wouldn't rate time on TV.

She still looked shocked and a little frightened when she asked her question: "Does it . . . have any connection with the work he was doing for us?"

"I don't know what that work was," I told her. "Not yet."

Before she could say anything to that, Yann Bouvier came into the room. She looked at him, and then looked quickly

away and put on her glasses. Color had mounted in her
cheeks. It would have been called a blush back in the days
when they did such things.

"Susan wants to see you now," Bouvier told me, and
motioned to Carmen Haung. "She'd like you there, too, Carmen."

I followed them out of the room. There was more than
enough width to the hallway for Carmen Haung to walk beside the mason who'd become Susan Kape's companion-
driver-bodyguard—as well as probable lover and possible
husband-to-be. But she didn't. She stayed half a step behind
him, all the way.

8

UNLIKE THE PARTS OF THE BUILDING DESTINED TO BECOME the Simon Kape Museum, there was nothing incomplete about the right wing. Its wide hall had a goodly supply of gilt and white Chippendale furniture, softly lit by eighteenth-century crystal chandeliers, and its walls were paneled and hung with old Gobelins tapestries.

Another change was the heating. It was turned up higher than in the other two sections. I unbuttoned my jacket and let it hang open. The Beretta remained unseen in a holster clipped to the back of my belt. I followed Yann Bouvier and Carmen Haung into the room where Susan Kape was waiting for us.

Coming out of the hall, it was like stepping into another century. Into this century, but not this decade. The room was a curious mix of Art Nouveau and Deco.

Diffused light came through panels of sandblasted glass with sharp-angled designs that covered much of one wall. Across from it hung a big, richly colored tapestry with sinuously curving peacock patterns. In front of that was a mobile bar—an extravaganza of rosewood and brass with an opened rolltop and black tile sink.

The most eye-catching furnishing dominated another wall—one of those cherrywood bookcases sculpted by Rupert Carabin. Its shelves were full of books with old leather bindings, but nobody was likely to get around to noticing their gold-embossed titles. There was too much distraction in Carabin's sensuous, full-figured nudes, cavorting uninhibitedly across the top of the bookcase and down its sides.

In fact, the only thing in the room that would draw one's gaze away from that bookcase was Susan Kape.

Her white silk blouse and loose-flowing orange skirt clung softly to a figure as voluptuous as Carabin's daydreams. Her gently curling auburn hair framed a face with long, large dark eyes and plump lips that repeated the promise of her figure.

But dealing with pain had dug deeper lines into that face than was normal for a woman who still had a couple years to go before she turned thirty.

She sat on a starkly functional swivel chair of naked steel and black leather. Her shoes, as always now, were flat-heeled. Against the mobile bar next to her leaned a pair of padded metal crutches.

According to the last account I'd read, Susan Kape had so far been in for three extensive operations, and whether she would ever walk again without those crutches remained questionable.

And yet neither being crippled, nor the marks it had left on her, detracted from the power of the erotic allure Susan Kape exuded. There was nothing delicate or ethereal about her. She simmered with carnal energy and was accustomed to men responding to it.

I was damn sure she registered *my* response to it from the moment she took my hand in polite greeting and looked into my eyes.

There was a man sitting on her other side in a suede-covered club chair. Tall and thin, in his midsixties, with a dark, sternly distinguished face. Susan Kape introduced him as the chief of her company's legal department: Piercarlo Petulla.

His face relaxed into a surprisingly friendly smile. It positively twinkled. "I don't think we should start calling each other by our first names, do you?" The only flaw in his English was the Harvard accent.

"Not unless we want to form a nightclub act." My smile wasn't as accomplished as his. Twinkling isn't my strong point.

"Pete and Pete." His chuckle was pretty good, too.

None of it meant Piercarlo Petulla had decided to adopt me. It was insurance charm. Establishing a matey rapport in case some future development required me to choose sides. Lawyers don't get to be members of the board without hedging all bets. He could ooze surface warmth, but it was cold as marble inside. You could see it in the pinched nostrils of the long, down-slanted nose tip.

Susan Kape had given him a hard look, but her tone remained mild. "Please, Piercarlo, let's keep this conversation in French. I don't want Yann feeling like a piece of furniture."

The twinkle left his expression instantly, and the stern dignity was back. "My apologies," he said in flawless French. "I forgot that Monsieur Bouvier hasn't yet grasped the English language."

Yann Bouvier didn't say a thing. He leaned against the side of the doorway, folded his arms across his broad chest, and gazed coldly at a space slightly above Piercarlo Petulla's distinguished, balding head.

Carmen Haung lowered herself stiffly into another suede club chair, her face tensed and her slender hands clenching on her lap.

Susan Kape looked back to me and pointed to a third club chair facing her. "Won't you sit down, Monsieur Sawyer. We didn't expect you to come to Paris first. Monsieur Donhoff thought you'd fly directly to Rome. As a matter of fact, I called him about an hour ago, trying to confirm that. But since you're here—"

She was cut short by Carmen Haung, who couldn't hold

it back any longer. She blurted out what I'd told her about Fritz getting shot on Saturday night.

Researchers have counted over a thousand subtle variations of emotion that can be expressed by the nerve-muscle complex of any normal face. That makes it very difficult to judge if someone's reactions are genuine or faked. Trying to identify minute shifts between one facial signal and another close to it—when you're watching *three* people at the same time—multiplies the problem. I've spent years working on how to do it. As a Chicago cop, a federal narc, and then a Senate investigator abroad before going private. It never gets easy.

But each of the three—Susan Kape, Piercarlo Petulla, and Yann Bouvier—appeared to be as startled as Carmen Haung had been.

The first to speak was Petulla. "How is he now?" he asked me with more emotion than a stranger would be expected to show out of polite concern.

"Still unconscious. Still in intensive care. But he'll come through, given time."

"I *hope* so," Petulla said in what seemed like some kind of anger. Against himself, it developed. "I'm the one responsible for getting Fritz involved in whatever it is."

"Sounds as if you know Fritz pretty well."

"Since long before you ever met him," Petulla told me. "My father was prominent in anti-Fascist politics in Milan. Mussolini had him arrested and later deported to Germany, where he'd vanished by the war's end. It turned out he suffered head injuries that impaired his memory. Fritz Donhoff helped me find him. Later, in the fifties, he was able to help us with certain company problems. So when *this* problem of Susan's came up, I naturally turned to Fritz."

Petulla shook his head somberly. "I should have realized, he's not young enough anymore to take on something that could turn dangerous. But I didn't *expect*—"

"Just a moment," Susan Kape interrupted. "We don't

know as yet that what happened to Monsieur Donhoff has anything to do with me." She looked to me. "*Do* we?"

She wore a ring on the middle finger of her right hand, and she had a nervous habit of twisting the ring around her finger. She was doing that now, without realizing it, as our eyes met again.

"*I* don't," I told her. "Because I still don't know anything about the job you handed him."

"Let me explain," Petulla said. "The art world is, as I'm sure you know, full of opportunists of every sort, including just plain thieves. I wanted to make sure that Susan here wasn't about to get herself involved with someone of that ilk who might be attempting—"

"Hold on," I said, hard enough to stop him. "You're jumping into the middle of it. I want to get it in sequence from the beginning."

Petulla was about to speak again, but Susan Kape held up a hand, its flattened palm toward him. A startlingly imperious gesture. Reminding one that while she was used to letting others handle many things for her—because she chose to—she was also accustomed to obedience without having to struggle for it.

"I'll tell it," she said without undue emphasis. "It is my problem, *if* there is a problem."

Petulla shut his mouth, biting down on whatever he'd begun to say.

Yann Bouvier looked at him directly for the first time, smiling just a little.

Carmen Haung shot a glance in Bouvier's direction, and then looked away toward the bookcase. She seemed to concentrate on it, as if trying to learn how to become like the Carabin nudes cavorting so unashamedly around it.

Keeping watch on all of them at the same time wasn't getting any easier. Especially with the added difficulty I was having in looking at anything in that room except Susan Kape.

She exercised a potent pull on a man. Her nervous tension was an ingredient, along with her absolute confidence.

But looking at her too much made my fingers curl with the urge to touch. And she remained aware of it, no matter how intent she was about everything she had to say.

"If you want it from the beginning," she told me, "you need to understand some things about this museum I'm trying to create. With Carmen's help," she added, with a nod at her antiquities expert. "But I'm not completely ignorant about ancient art myself. I did major in it at the University of Pennsylvania."

"You caught your father's interest in it," I suggested.

"Not really. Though it was mostly to please him that I did it. That's where I met Carmen, at Penn. We were taking the same major. Except she was dead serious about it, of course. Me—I dropped it and forgot it, the day I graduated."

Her half-rueful smile felt, at my end of it, like she was staking a claim to some kind of emotional complicity between us. I didn't give it too much weight. She probably did that to all the boys. But it jumped my blood pressure nonetheless.

I looked away to Carmen Haung. "And you continued with it."

"Well, *I* had a living to make." Her glance at Susan Kape was an uncomfortable blend of wry and apologetic. "I'd had to work in a diner nights to put myself through those first four years. Then I stayed on at Penn going for my doctorate. Squeaking by financially on a scholarship loan. Plus what I could earn by teaching, and then doing research and cataloguing for the university's archeological museum. They have a good one."

"Yes, I know." Babette had spent a semester as guest professor at the University of Pennsylvania.

"And after that I got a job in New York, at Galton-Stallbrass. The auction house?"

"On Madison, behind the Stanhope."

"You've been there?"

"I did some work involving their Chinese art department one time," I said. "What did you do there?"

"I was an assistant to its director of ancient art and artifacts."

I didn't have any idea if what she was telling me was going to be of any help to me. But the chance some part of it would prove useful somewhere along the line was worth the slow, piecemeal raking through seemingly irrelevant information.

"But the two of you kept in touch," I said.

It was Susan Kape who responded. "No, never. We hadn't been close friends, just classmates. After I left school Carmen was into real work. While I was off, flitting around. *Flitting*—that's the right word for it."

She paused and gave me just a suggestion of a smile this time. The slightest deepening at the corners of her ripe mouth. Nobody else in the room seemed aware of the electricity passing between us. But it was there.

"I never was interested in joining my father's business," she continued. "And at that point in my life I couldn't seem to get serious about anything else. Except having fun. And usually making a mess of that. I assume you know all that. The syndicated slime-slingers had a field day with me."

I knew what most people who read the papers knew. Young heiress Susan Kape and her latest romances, either starting or ending. They seemed to bloom and die as fast as she did the circuit of the in-crowd's party places. Palm Beach to Monaco to New York to Gstaad. She'd gotten her second divorce the year she celebrated her twenty-third birthday, with what the society pages gushed over as "the most fabulous party of the Paris season."

She looked toward Yann Bouvier. "I didn't begin to settle down until after I met Yann."

He smiled at her. There was affection in it, but some uncertainty, too. "You mean after your accident."

"Well, yes, that, too, of course." The ring she was twisting around her finger had a big cabochon sapphire set in a base of diamonds. There were smaller matching sapphires in the cuff links of her blouse and attached to the plump lobes of her smallish ears. I figured the ring alone would run almost half a million dollars, and found myself glancing from it to her crutches.

She looked down at her hands, saw what she was doing, and made herself stop it, placing her hands on the arms of her steel and leather swivel chair. "I guess the idea of creating a museum in honor of my father first began germinating in the back of my head when he died. I got a letter from Carmen. A very sympathetic letter, offering her condolences. And then suggesting that if I was interested in disposing of Daddy's collection, Galton-Stallbrass could almost certainly auction it for more money than anyone else."

Carmen Haung grimaced. "I *hated* writing that letter. But all auction houses are hearse chasers by nature. Each of them has somebody whose job it is to go through the new obituaries every day. And people there knew I'd been to school with Susan. So it was *suggested* I contact her."

"I refused, of course," Susan Kape said. "It would have felt like treason, getting rid of all my father spent so much of his life gathering. I'm not in the position of most people who have to sell off things left by their ancestors. I don't need the money. But I still didn't know *what* I was going to do with his collection."

She patted her knees, not fondly. "Until this happened to me. And I had to do some straight, hard thinking about what I was going to occupy myself with for the rest of my life."

"You decided running a museum might do it."

"Yes. I lured Carmen away from Galton-Stallbrass to help me organize it. But one thing she soon made me realize. Turning Daddy's collection into a museum is going to be more complicated than I originally thought."

"As well as," Petulla slipped in drily, "much more expensive. Not," he added quickly, "that the company's board of directors will hesitate for a moment to contribute whatever is needed."

I'd been checking out Yann Bouvier from time to time during this conversation. He was listening, but not with deep interest. Susan Kape wanted him there, but I could see he felt his presence didn't mean anything one way or the other.

"You see," Carmen Haung was explaining to me, "while Susan's father did make some excellent purchases, he didn't go about it systematically. Just bought whatever he happened to like. There are large gaps. More has to be acquired before anyone in the field would regard a museum based on his collection as anything more than just a rich man's hobby."

"Which," Susan Kape said tightly, "his daughter should contribute to an existing museum. Or sell off at auction. Instead of trying to inflate it beyond its real worth."

"Getty's collection was just a rich man's hobby," I said. "The museum *he* left is regarded pretty highly."

Carmen Haung leaned forward in her club chair, intent on making her point. "Because Getty's trustees added to that collection with some very spectacular buys. So spectacular it forced everyone to take the Getty seriously."

"That's what *I* need here," Susan Kape told me. There was an edge of obsession in her voice. "Something spectacular enough to make the whole damned art world sit up and take notice. Well, last week a dealer approached me with an offer—an extremely secretive offer—of a chance to get my hands on a treasure that would *do* that. A fabulous find, that no one has seen for over two thousand years."

She was twisting that sapphire ring again.

"Who is the dealer?" I asked her.

"Friedhelm Dollinger," she told me.

"Jesus Christ," I said.

9

"*My* sentiments exactly," Piercarlo Petulla told me. "After Susan informed me of Dollinger's approach to her I did a preliminary check on his reputation."

"He's a crook," I said.

Susan Kape's expression had become resistant. "I don't believe he's ever been arrested on any charge. Let alone sent to prison."

"What some people know about Freddie Dollinger is one thing," I told her. "What a court of law could prove is another."

"He *is* a rather shady character," Carmen Haung said. "That's why I agreed with Monsieur Petulla that we should hire someone qualified to investigate. To make sure Dollinger isn't attempting some sort of swindle on us."

"He's pulled off more than a few of those," I said. "Smooth as ice. A gifted con man, among his other talents."

"I know that. *But* Friedhelm Dollinger has also been the intermediary in some entirely legitimate deals between the sellers and buyers of some extraordinary finds. Such as the Aidin treasure now in New York's Metropolitan Museum of Art."

"The legitimacy of the Met's possession of that Aidin silver is debatable," I reminded her. "It's stolen goods."

Susan Kape was the one who objected to that. "*Stolen—* that's a question of semantics."

"It was looted from a tomb in Turkey," I said. "Smuggled illegally out of Turkey to the States. Turkey is demanding its return."

"It won't be returned," Carmen Haung said emphatically. "Why should it be? Those works in silver were created by the Byzantine civilization, which no longer exists. The Turks defeated Byzantium in war and crushed it out of existence. So what right do the Turks have to that treasure? The right of the victorious conqueror?"

I didn't argue the point. Too many people had argued over it for too many centuries. Who did an ancient treasure belong to? The present government of the land in which it was unearthed, or those who found it, or those who bought and cherished it?

So far the most eminently respectable gentlemen of the multibillion-dollar world of art continue to incline toward two unwritten legal standards: possession is nine-tenths of the law and finders keepers.

I looked at Piercarlo Petulla. "So you hired Fritz to check on whether Dollinger does have something worth buying in this case, or if he's trying to run a hoax."

"I thought it necessary," Petulla said, "considering the amount of money involved. Susan and Carmen agreed, though they insisted any investigation be carried out with delicate care. According to this man Dollinger, the arrangement would fall through if the existence of the treasure becomes known before Susan is in possession of it."

"How much is he asking for this treasure?"

"Eighteen million dollars."

"That's money," I agreed.

"It's worth every penny," Susan Kape said. "The Japanese paid almost forty million dollars for just one Van Gogh. For the same reason as those big Getty buys: to get attention and respect. What I'm being offered will cost half that and has much more intrinsic value."

"What's Freddie Dollinger offering you?"

Susan Kape hesitated.

I said, "You must have told Fritz Donhoff about it."

"Yes, but Piercarlo vouched for his integrity and discretion."

Petulla spoke up for me. "From what Fritz Donhoff has told me about his young partner, you can trust *him* just as much." He gave me another of his smiles, less twinkly but chock-full of sincere regard.

Susan Kape told me, "Monsieur Dollinger is acting as go-between for some people—whose identities he won't reveal—who have found an Etruscan tomb. Filled with the treasures that were placed inside it when the family who owned the tomb were buried there. A wealthy and distinguished family."

"Most of those tombs were looted long ago," I said.

"Yes," Carmen Haung said, "starting with pillaging by the Romans who wiped out the Etruscans and all evidence of their civilization that was above ground. But no looters ever discovered *this* tomb."

"Until now."

If there was anything sardonic in the way I said that, Susan Kape appeared not to notice. "All the treasure of that tomb is *intact*," she said with barely contained excitement. "We've seen color photographs taken inside the burial vault. Everything—the works of gold, silver, stone, clay—they're in mint condition, after more than twenty centuries."

"That could be worth the price," I admitted. "If it's authentic."

"Dollinger lent us two pieces from the tomb. A bronze mirror engraved with the figure of the river god Achelous and a ceramic pitcher decorated with a nymph and a satyr. I had Carmen take them to a friend of mine at the Louvre for scientific examination."

I looked to Carmen Haung. "Spectrographic testing?"

"*Everything,*" she told me. "Ceramic analysis, thermoluminescence, and archaeomagnetism dating—"

"They *are* authentic," Susan Kape interrupted with absolute conviction. "Carmen was sure they were, and the tests confirmed it."

"That doesn't guarantee the rest of what Dollinger delivers will be."

"That's why I'm going to Rome," Carmen Haung told me. "To examine the rest of it. Monsieur Donhoff felt it would be safer to have you there with me. I agreed."

"Is that where this treasure is now?" I asked her. "In Rome?"

"No, it's still in the tomb they found. They'll contact me in Rome and take me—and you—to it. I don't know *where* the tomb is. Except that it must be someplace between Rome and Florence, since all the lost Etruscan cities were in that area. I have a feeling Monsieur Dollinger doesn't know the exact location of the tomb either."

That was possible, even probable. Tomb robbers needed a middleman who had contacts among potential buyers with the kind of cash they wanted for their find. But telling a slippery dealer like Freddie Dollinger where the tomb was would be an invitation to him to rifle it before they did.

"Dollinger *knows* I'll be coming with you?"

Carmen Haung nodded. "We told him on Friday, after Monsieur Donhoff suggested it."

"Was he aware he was being investigated?"

"No, I'm fairly sure not. We didn't even tell him your name. Just that I'd feel safer taking a bodyguard with me. He said it wasn't necessary, but he agreed to it."

"Will Dollinger be there in Rome?"

"I think so."

"Is he already down there, or still here in Paris?"

"I don't know. We could phone his place and—"

"*Don't* phone him. Just give me his address. He was

changing them pretty often the last time I had dealings with him.''

She gave it to me: an apartment on the Quai de Montebello.

Now *that* was interesting. Friedhelm Dollinger's place was only a block and a half from Place Maubert, and the bottom of the street where Fritz had been shot.

I asked Susan Kape, ''How did Dollinger contact you originally? Directly or through someone else?''

''He got in touch with Carmen first. She brought him to me.''

''He came to *me* with what he had,'' Carmen Haung explained, ''because of the treasure being Etruscan. That's my special field of expertise—Etruscology. Monsieur Dollinger knew that somehow.''

''Knowing facts like that is one of the things that keeps him solvent.'' I turned to Yann Bouvier, who continued to stand against the side of the doorway, looking bored. ''Did *you* ever meet Dollinger?'' I asked him.

''Yes. Once, when Carmen brought him to talk to Susan.''

''What do you think?''

He was surprised to have anyone in that room ask for his opinion. It took him a moment. ''*I* think he's not someone I want Susan associated with. I think he is dragging her into the twilight world, between dog and wolf. A world of shadows and danger. What has happened to Monsieur Donhoff proves I was right.''

''But *I'm* not going to do anything dangerous,'' Susan Kape said.

I said, ''There are other dangers besides the possibility of getting shot. The Italian government takes a dim view of having its national treasures lifted.''

''This is not *Italian* treasure,'' Susan Kape said fiercely. ''It belonged to the Etruscans, who no longer exist and were no more related to present-day Italians than they were to their enemies, the Romans.''

I didn't care to get into another "finders keepers" discussion. "Right or wrong," I said, "the Italian police regard removing things from a tomb that happens to be in their country as a crime. Burglary, plus expropriating part of their nation's heritage. And then it'll have to be slipped out of Italy and brought here. That's called smuggling.''

"But I won't be physically involved with either of those *criminal* acts," Susan Kape pointed out calmly. "And once it is *here*, I doubt very much that the Italian government will succeed in taking it away from me.''

Piercarlo Petulla was nodding judiciously. "One must expect that there will be some loud screams from south of the border, of course. Reproaches and demands. But nothing that can't be handled. And the notoriety *would* increase everyone's interest in the museum that acquired this find.''

Nine-tenths of the law . . .

I asked him, "*When* did you hire Fritz to check on Dollinger and his deal?''

"Just this last Thursday.''

"Did he report anything to you between then and when he was gunned down on Saturday night?''

"No. I assumed it was too soon for him to have anything to report.''

I decided it was time to spring another name on them, while their minds were occupied elsewhere. "How is Arnaud Galice involved in this?''

They all looked blank.

I pushed the name around a bit more, but it didn't appear to mean a thing to any of them.

I left quickly after that. It was past midnight by then. I had something to do before it got much later.

As I got up to leave I took another look at Susan Kape. She was looking back at me. No smile at all this time. I thought I detected something quizzical—or maybe challenging—in her big dark eyes. But I could have been mistaken. Hers weren't the kind of eyes you could drown in. They didn't let you get in deep enough.

🔲 **10** 🔲

THE FLOODLAMPS ILLUMINATING NOTRE DAME HAD BEEN turned off at midnight. The dark cathedral spires pointed into a night sky where stars glistened like bits of ice. The mist blowing over the river had a raw chill. It wasn't a Chicago-brand cold. The thermometer never drops that low in Paris, and the wind never reaches Lake Michigan velocity. But it was cold enough to make me shiver.

I'd been spending too much time in mild winters along the Riviera. If a Paris December could make me want to button my topcoat, I wouldn't survive an hour in an ordinary Illinois snowstorm.

I did button it, but not until I'd taken the gun out of my belt holster and transferred it to the topcoat's right-hand pocket. Then I walked away from my car, along the dark, deserted Quai de Montebello to Friedhelm Dollinger's address.

It was in one of the tall, narrow houses that look across the left branch of the Seine at the Ile de la Cité. From the house you could see past Notre Dame to the hospital where Fritz was pitting whatever reserves he had left against his old enemy, Death.

Dollinger's apartment was on the second floor front. Looking up from the sidewalk, I saw lights on behind its windows. It seemed I was in luck. But that thought wasn't destined to last long.

The house door had a panel of numbered buttons next to it. You had to punch the right combination to open the lock. I didn't know the combination. But one of the windows up there was open. I stepped back and called, "Dollinger! I have to talk to you!"

There was no response. When I'd waited long enough I upped my volume. "Come on, Dollinger, let me in! I'm not going away until we talk!"

A man poked his head out of a dark window above Dollinger's apartment. "Are you crazy, making all that noise?" he shouted at me. "Don't you realize what time it is?"

"You want to sleep," I yelled back, "make your downstairs neighbor open up!"

"I'll call the police!"

"Fine—*they'll* make him come down and unlock this door!"

A woman's head appeared in Dollinger's open window. She looked very young. Much too young for Freddie Dollinger. Unless she was his granddaughter, and as far as I knew he'd reached the round age of sixty without burdening himself with family anywhere along the route. He travels most furtively who travels alone.

"Monsieur Dollinger isn't home," she called down to me. "He's gone away—a business trip."

"Then I'll talk to you. Come down and let me in."

"No! Go away! Please!" She sounded scared.

"It's up to you," I told her. "Come down or I kick in the door and come up."

She came down.

Her torso leaned all the way out the window and then the rest of her followed it.

She did a half somersault in midair as she dropped. Her back struck the sidewalk next to me with a crunch that threatened to turn my stomach inside out.

Her eyes stared up at me when I crouched over her. I started to feel for her pulse but then saw I needn't bother.

It wasn't normal. The window she'd come out of wasn't high enough for the fall to kill her instantly. Unless she'd cracked her head open.

I turned her over.

There was a knife hilt protruding from her back.

The hilt had been twisted to one side by the impact with the paving, but the blade was still deep inside. The job had been done by someone with a knowledge of anatomy and a sure hand. The knife had been driven between her vertebrae at exactly the right spot to pierce her heart.

11

THE MAN IN THE APARTMENT ABOVE DOLLINGER'S HAD ducked back inside. By now he'd be on the phone to the cops, but I couldn't wait for them to get there. I *wanted* to wait. Because if the skilled killer up there was the woman who'd taken a split second to shoot Paul Dupuy in the head and heart last night, I didn't relish going in against her.

But I did go in.

Not fast. First there was the door. It took two hard kicks to bust the lock loose from the frame. Then there was the light inside the entry. Someone had pushed the timer button turning it on. Holding my Beretta pistol ready, I stayed just outside the doorway until the light flicked off. Then I went through the dark entry and up the stairway, quietly. Quiet means slow. I was halfway up the stairs when I heard a noise at the rear end of the corridor up there.

I looked both ways before taking the last three steps to the top. At the front end of the corridor the door of Dollinger's apartment was wide open and the lights were on inside it. At the rear end of the corridor there was a window, also wide open. I went there first.

The rear window looked down into a small courtyard containing nothing but some garbage cans, and entirely enclosed by the backs of buildings. There were murky openings to two covered alleyways down there. One cut through the block

65

toward Rue de Bièvre, the other in the direction of Place Maubert. The window wasn't too high for someone to jump down and go off through either alley. Providing he or she landed feet first, with good balance, and without a knife in the back.

I went toward the front of the corridor fairly certain the killer was gone. But I didn't stroll into Dollinger's apartment. I dove in, doing two fast rolls across the floor with my teeth clenched. Clenching your teeth won't make bullets bounce off you. But it helps you control the shock, like preparing yourself to get alcohol poured into an open cut.

The only shock I got was when my second roll knocked over a little table. The delicate Chinese vase that had been on top of it exploded into a hundred pieces on the floor beside me. I stood up and looked around. I was in Dollinger's living room. It was crowded with antique furniture, costly knick-knacks, and works by master sculptors and painters—or clever replicas of all of these. Or maybe a combination of the two.

I went through a connecting hall to the room from which the murdered girl had fallen. It was a large, ornate bedroom. A clothes closet was open and so was a drawer of what was either a Louis Quinze bureau or a very good imitation of one. A suitcase was open on the canopied bed. The suitcase was half-filled with women's clothes and cosmetics, dumped in hastily. It looked like the girl had been packing to leave when she'd been interrupted—by the killer or by me.

I left the apartment and went back down the stairway swiftly, strode half a block to my parked Renault. After the pistol that I had no right to carry was safely back in its hiding place I walked another block to a public telephone. I heard the first police car approaching as I dialed Commissaire Gojon's number.

The ability to get by on very little sleep is a prime asset for any investigator, public or private. On occasion it can be as useful as a good memory, the plodding perseverance of a turtle, and a strong stomach. Generally three hours' sleep a night can carry me through a couple days, before the brain and legs begin stalling and I have to sack out for ten or twelve to restore optimum function. So I was okay at 8:30 A.M. although I hadn't gotten to bed until after four.

It had been almost three in the morning when I'd finished dictating my version of the girl's murder to one of Gojon's BRI inspectors and signed all the typed copies. Then I had coffee with Commissaire Gojon while we pushed some theories around. We didn't have enough facts at that point to make it worth the effort.

All we knew about the dead girl was that her name was Lucette Majorelle and she'd been eighteen when she died (according to the French ID card found on her); and she'd been Friedhelm Dollinger's live-in girlfriend for the past five months (according to neighbors). The police hadn't found anything in Dollinger's apartment that related to Etruscan treasure or that gave a clue to his present whereabouts.

I set a luncheon appointment with Gojon for noon to find out if anything further had surfaced by then. That would leave me enough time to meet Carmen Haung and board our flight to Rome.

Nobody was waiting in ambush for me at my apartment. I put through two overseas phone calls, one to Philadelphia and the other to New York. The difference in time zones made it 10:30 P.M. there. Both parties I wanted to talk to were at home. I told each what I wanted, and then set the alarm and got ready for bed. But that last coffee with Gojon hadn't been a good idea. I lay there with my eyes wide open, trying, once again, to come up with answers to the questions:

Why had somebody shot Fritz?

Why had a thug named Paul Dupuy been killed in Fritz's apartment, and a girl named Lucette Majorelle been killed in Freddie Dollinger's place?

What connection was there between the job Fritz was doing for Susan Kape and his sudden interest in Arnaud Galice, an information peddler who was supposed to have died in Istanbul two years ago?

One thing I was fairly sure of. Fritz hadn't been shot just to stop him from checking on Dollinger. Killing Fritz, Dollinger was bright enough to realize, would only focus more attention on the investigation.

The explanation had to lie somewhere among the answers to the other questions. And I couldn't come up with any I'd bet on. So finally I forced my eyes shut and dragged myself down into temporary oblivion. Using the old reliable Sawyer simulation method. Imagine swimming out to sea. A warm Mediterranean, way out there with the big, lazy round-topped waves. Count each high swell as it takes you up and down, up and down. . . .

The alarm jangled me awake. Half an hour got me shaved, showered, and dressed, with instant coffee inside me and my overnight bag packed. I carried the bag down to my car, tossed it in back, and drove to the Hôtel Dieu on the Seine's big island.

I got there on time. The doctor in charge of Fritz's case was making his morning rounds.

"He regained consciousness a couple times last night," he told me. "Not for long, and not sufficiently to speak intelligibly. But I do think we can say he is finally on his way to recovery, barring unexpected setbacks. But that doesn't mean," he warned, "that you have permission to question him if he wakes again while you're visiting him. I don't want him subjected to that sort of strain yet."

Fritz didn't look any better to me. But most French doctors won't give you an optimistic prognosis until they're sure they won't be proved wrong, and I was more than willing to accept this one. I stood looking down at Fritz for a while, and then I stood at the window for a longer while gazing out and running last night's questions through my head again. Daylight didn't bring any clearer answers.

Some snowflakes were beginning to drift in the misty breeze outside. Across the water people were rushing to grab the last available taxicabs along the Right Bank before the snow came down in earnest. On the parapet there a bookseller who didn't believe the snow would last was opening up her stall to catch early browsers. The first tour boat of the morning made impatient noises at a tug maneuvering a heavy bargeload of smashed automobiles around the Ile de la Cité.

Behind me, Fritz said something that sounded like "Harrrumph . . ."

I turned and went back to his bed. His eyes were open. Dopey, but open. The bags under them did look less deflated.

When I leaned over him, he smiled a little and said, "How are you, my boy?"

"Not bad, you old bastard." My voice wasn't as steady as I'd have wanted. "Considering the hard time you've been giving me."

It was like that between us. I'd never had a father and he'd never had children.

In spite of the doctor's warning there was one question I had to ask him. I started to. But Fritz went back to sleep in the middle of it.

When I left the hospital, I dropped into the nearest bistro and had a real coffee to keep all systems on Go. A double *express*, with two still-warm croissants and a little *tarte aux pommes*. Then I drove off the Ile de la Cité over Pont St. Michel and angled across Montparnasse to burgle my mother's office.

⊠ **12** ⊠

BABETTE WAS AWAY THAT MONTH DOING RESEARCH AT THE Museum of Western Asiatic Antiquity in East Berlin. The office where she did most of her writing was on Boulevard Raspail, two blocks from her apartment. It didn't take much work with a lockpick to let myself in. The lock was a simple one. There wasn't anything a normal thief would consider worth stealing. Only the books and papers of her profession.

From her two office windows you could see, if you wanted to, the top third of the Montparnasse Tower. A blot on the view from half the windows of Paris. Erected because President Pompidou had wanted to be remembered for having built the tallest office building in Europe, along with some other architectural monstrosities.

Parisians learn to pretend it isn't there.

I looked instead at Babette's bookcases. She had her faults, but disorder was not one of them. The books on the Etruscans were neatly together on one shelf. Not taking up much space, because not much is known about the Etruscans. I went through the most up-to-date book, full of color photographs, to familiarize myself with the look of recent finds. Then I took down what I really wanted: George Dennis's *Cities and Cemeteries of Etruria*.

That wasn't up-to-date. Dennis wrote it in the middle of the last century. But it remains the most thorough introduc-

70

tion to the subject. Babette had the Dent edition of 1907. Two pocket-sized volumes, which suited me fine. I slipped them into the side pockets of my topcoat, let myself out, and relocked her door.

I'd make sure the books were back in place on their shelf before she returned from East Berlin. Babette has her good points, but a tolerant attitude about people who borrow anything from her without prior permission is not one of them. Borrowing anything from her *with* permission isn't too easy either.

From her office it was a short walk to the place where Commissaire Gojon was to join me for lunch. And that Right Bank bookseller's feel for Paris weather had been correct. The snow had vanished after its one teasing feint at the city's nerves. I turned into Boulevard du Montparnasse at Rodin's powerful statue of Balzac. That brought me into the short block with the four bistros that form the spiritual hub of the quarter. The Rotonde, Dôme, Coupole, and Select.

Each tends to draw a different breed of clientele. Famous faces, urbane business types, and tourists with a generous supply of traveler's checks prefer the classy spaciousness of the Coupole. The modest-sized Select, across the boulevard from it, gets a scruffier lot. I went in there.

A mixed bag of Select habitués had already laid claim to half the tables. University students debating heatedly over coffees. Chess players munching prelunch snacks while they worked out killer moves. Artists and intellectuals who considered serious drinking essential to serious thought, getting a long head start on a self-imposed task that, come night, they would call "holding back the dawn."

Feeling at home in the Select was one of Commissaire Gojon's perversities.

He wasn't due there for another hour. That gave me time to cull some basic information about Etruscan tombs from the two volumes I'd borrowed from Babette. But first I used the telephone next to the Select's toilets.

I made three long-distance calls. Each to a different number in Rome.

Then I took a rear table, ordered a tall *citron pressé*, and began dipping into Volume One.

I was into its speculation about claims that the Etruscans were a shamelessly lecherous people when Gojon showed up. He draped his coat neatly over the back of the chair facing me before he sat down. He had changed clothes and was freshly shaved. I doubted that he'd had any sleep since I'd last seen him. The only sign of it was behind the lenses of his black-rimmed glasses. His eyes were bloodshot.

A waiter came to our table with a promptness the Select's customers don't normally expect. The staff knew what Gojon was. He ordered a *croque-madame* with an extra egg and a *demi*. I was hungrier than that. I took the *paupiettes de veau* with potatoes and salad and a small pitcher of rosé. The waiter hurried away and Gojon said, "We haven't been able to locate Friedhelm Dollinger."

"Have you asked Interpol to put out a bulletin on him?"

"My superiors," Gojon said drily, "don't feel that is justified at this early stage. He isn't charged with any crime. As yet. And he's not wanted as a witness to the girl's murder, because he wasn't there at the time. At least, we have no evidence that he was. Although he *could* be the one who killed her."

"Freddie Dollinger is too old, fat, and slow to jump out that back window that fast. And he's never used a knife for anything more deadly than spreading butter on his toast. Anything on the girl?"

"Her parents have a *boulangerie* up in Longwy. She left home at fifteen. Worked as a clerk in a number of Paris shops until she met Dollinger. Her employers say she was honest and competent, but too inclined to flirt with well-off customers. She didn't have any criminal connections, as far as we've been able to learn. And that is all we have—on her or anything else connected with her murder.''

"Except," I said, "she was throwing all her things into a suitcase before she was killed."

"Yes. Until something comes up that proves us wrong, the sequence of events you and I worked out still holds. Someone came to Dollinger's place to take the girl away before you or others could ask her questions. But you showed up too soon. Making it difficult for that someone to slip the girl out."

"And easier to silence her with a knife."

"All of which sounds right," Gojon said, "but it's still only guesswork."

"You don't have much else at this point."

"Not much," Gojon agreed, with a bit of edge in his tone. He fell silent as the waiter came with our meals. When we were alone again he said, "I might have more to go on if you would explain what it is you're doing for Susan Kape, and what Monsieur Donhoff was doing for her before you."

"I *told* you what I could. She wants to find out if Dollinger is trying to swindle her. The details are confidential. She wouldn't like it if I revealed them. Or if you put pressure on me to. Of course," I added, with a certain amount of relish, "you *could* go and ask her about it yourself. I did suggest that, remember. Have you tried?"

Gojon concentrated on his croque madame as though he hadn't heard the question. He had once gone into a building after a madman who was armed with an ax and holding a child hostage. Gojon had taken him barehanded. But we both knew he didn't have the kind of nerve required to go in against someone like Susan Kape. Not without first having sufficient justification to get written authority to do so, from much higher up the ladder. If he annoyed Susan Kape on his own authority, Piercarlo Petulla and his legal staff would shred Gojon's career potential into very small and bloody pieces.

Actually, I didn't give a damn about preserving the secrecy

of Susan Kape's confidential deal. Nor about the possibility of some hard-working swindlers gouging a dishonest buck out of her company. It's hard to get upset about the financial problems of somebody who can be taken for eighteen million dollars without being hurt beyond repair.

But I did care about getting my hands on whoever had shot Fritz. And having Susan Kape back me up gave me a lot more leeway than I'd have without her.

But I wouldn't always have her behind me. And I didn't want Gojon nursing a grudge. "One thing," I told him. "I'm flying to Rome this afternoon on that confidential matter. If I find out anything useful there, I'll let you know about it when I get back."

He gave me a thoughtful look. "Think you'll run into Friedhelm Dollinger there?" he asked quietly.

"I don't know." That was fairly truthful. I couldn't be sure.

"If you do," Gojon said, "warn him that he'd better get in touch with me. Very soon."

"I will," I promised. "If I do see him."

I assumed I would. What I couldn't make any assumptions about was who he might have with him. It could turn out to include a spooky killer who was equally efficient with gun or knife. And I wasn't about to try smuggling a weapon of my own onto an international flight.

That's why I'd made one of those three phone calls to Rome.

▨ **13** ▨

THE PARIOLI DISTRICT OF ROME LACKS THE CLASSICAL AND medieval wonders that draw sightseers to other parts of the city. And it isn't quaint. The architecture is more reminiscent of Southern California than Italy's past. It is a clean, tranquil residential area for fairly well-off Romans who like their city living with a touch of suburban calm and without foreign crowds.

I got out of the taxi on Via Archimede, near the crest of a gentle hill. Below, the street descended between white apartment buildings softened by restrained amounts of greenery. Above, it curled into blocks of private homes with walled gardens. The sun was going down, but the air was still warm enough for me to be comfortable with only a tweed jacket over my shirt and a silk scarf around my neck.

Gianrico Chiodo's address was a small residential hotel that rented suites by the month. It was colder inside. Too much marble. It's plentiful and cheap in Italy, where wood is an imported luxury. Most of its forests were cut down long ago and never replanted. The flooring radiated an icy chill through the soles of my shoes.

I rode the two-person elevator from the little lobby up to the fourth floor and rang Gianrico's bell. The peephole in the door opened and a brown eye peered through at me. Gianrico's eyes were blue. I identified myself. The door was opened by a buxom brunette wearing a fuzzy red bolero top. Her belly button was exposed. So was a lot of nicely curved leg, between black spike-heeled sandals and a dungaree miniskirt with white lace flounces. Vulgar-cute, like Gianrico's previous mistress. And the one before that.

The suite was warmed by two electric radiators plugged into opposite walls. It had a large living room with a dining alcove at the far end. An open staircase led to a balcony bedroom. The hotel furniture was plain and solid, difficult to damage enough to make the next tenant complain. Gianrico, who'd been living there almost two years, had added a great many colorful cushions, a TV set with video attachment, and several big, framed movie posters.

His latest mistress jerked a thumb at the stairs. "He's up in the tub," she said with a Cockney accent, and went back to the TV. It was playing a videocassette of *The Cotton Club*. She stood swaying in front of the screen, silently mouthing the words to "Ill Wind" along with Lonette McKee.

I climbed the stairs and crossed the bedroom area. The door to the bathroom was open. Gianrico was inside taking a bubble bath. To be factual, only half of him was in there. The rest of him was in the bedroom.

The hotel's builders had completed the walls of the bathroom before they discovered it was too small to hold a bathtub. They didn't panic. Italian ingenuity has been honed over two thousand years of coping with disasters, from Hannibal's elephants to traffic jams that can bring circulation to a standstill for six hours. The builders simply cut a hole in the lower half of the wall separating the bathroom from the bedroom and shoved the tub partway through it. I'd seen Gianrico's legs stretched out under the bubbles on my way across the bedroom.

The part of him waiting for me in the bathroom included his handsome blond head. He grinned at me and said, "How's tricks?" His English had been picked up pimping for American movie people, back before the Dolce Vita soured and they all quit Rome.

I said, "What have you got for me, Johnny?"

"Have a look. Bedroom dresser, top drawer."

I found it under his shirts, snuggled into a suede-lined belt holster. A Hungarian FP 9mm automatic with a checkered walnut grip. The FÊG-Budapest version of the Browning Hi-Power. Under the shirts with it was its double-column magazine, fully loaded with thirteen rounds.

I slipped the gun out of the holster and checked it thoroughly. It was in good condition; not used too much, just enough so everything worked the way it was supposed to. Loading the magazine into it, I stuck the gun back in the holster and clipped it to my belt under my jacket. It hung right.

I went back into the bathroom and asked Gianrico, "Haven't you got anything else?"

"That's all I could find that's good. You only gave me a few hours. What's the matter?"

"The trigger needs too much squeeze. Like all Hungarian models. I might need it to shoot with, not for testing my strength."

"The trigger pull could be a problem," he said blandly. "For an amateur. Not for you. You're just trying to knock the price down, don't kid me."

"How much?"

Gianrico named a price. I offered half. He went down a notch. We settled at a figure we'd both known it would come to from the start.

I paid him, counting out the bills. He sat up in the bathroom half of the tub and recounted them, getting them wet. Gianrico didn't mind that. Wet or dry, he liked touching new money.

His girlfriend was still engrossed in the TV screen, dancing along with Gregory Hines now. I had another look at those legs as I went down the stairs. She turned her head and smiled at me, breaking her rhythm. But she was back in step when I let myself out.

Carmen Haung and I had an early dinner in her hotel room that night while we waited for a call from Dollinger and his tomb robbers. She was dressed for the sort of country the call was likely to take us into. A pair of loose-fitting Levi's, with thick-soled hiking shoes and a checked wool shirt. I had put a sleeveless sweater on under my jacket, but I'd left the topcoat in my room.

We were staying at the Hassler, at the top of the Spanish Steps. Both of our rooms had a view across half the roofs of Rome to the domes of St. Peter's and the Castel San Angelo, on the other side of the Tiber. Nothing but the best when you represented Susan Kape.

"They should have called by now," Carmen said tensely when we were finished with the meal and I was pouring cognac for us. "I'm getting worried, Peter."

We were on a first-name basis by then, and I'd explained that I preferred her calling me Peter or Pete. Pierre-Ange was perfectly acceptable on French lips, but with an American accent it stirred unpleasant memories. Too many schoolyard fights over it when I was growing up in Chicago. And a couple more brutal ones in the army.

"They'll call," I assured her. "They're not about to pass on the kind of money your boss is able to fork over."

"Unless Dollinger and his people have gotten a higher offer."

"Higher than eighteen million?"

"You didn't see Dollinger's photographs," Carmen said. "I did. A find like *that*—we've got to sew it up soon, before word of it leaks out and other bidders sneak in."

"If word of it leaks out at this stage of the game," I told her, "the gang you're negotiating with will have the law crawling all over their operation." I shook my head. "Dollinger and company already have a sweet deal set with you and Susan Kape. If their find's genuine, it's hot. They'll want to get rid of it and take off with their money without delays. So relax, they'll call.''

Carmen finished off her cognac. I poured her a second. She took a quick, nervous nip. I nursed my first one. I needed a clear head that night, not liquor confidence.

"What made you pick the Etruscans as your special interest?" I asked her.

She squinted at me for a moment. Her glasses were on the table between us. "Do you know anything at all about the Etruscans?"

"They ruled over central Italy," I said, "roughly the area of Tuscany. Before the Romans were a tribe worth noticing. They fought the Greeks and Phoenicians and held their own. Then the Romans got strong enough to fight them and smash them, leaving nothing but what was in their tombs. Which was a lot, because the Etruscans were rich and believed in taking the good things of life with them into an afterlife. But nobody's figured out yet how to read the writing they left behind. So all that's known about what they were comes from their enemies, the Greeks and Romans."

"Highly prejudiced mentions," Carmen said. "All unfavorable."

"Especially concerning the immorality of upper-class Etruscan wives."

"Because the Etruscans were the only ones of that time whose women enjoyed equal privileges."

"And equal fun."

Carmen smiled at me. She had a nice smile. "You can see it in their tomb paintings. The wives sharing the pleasures of banquets and dances with their husbands."

"Uh-huh. You can't get more debauched than that. Greek and Roman wives stayed where they belonged. At home. The *men* went to parties. With courtesans, who weren't immoral because they were practicing their profession."

Carmen shook an accusing finger at me. "You've been boning up on the subject!"

"I flipped through the Dennis work," I admitted.

"George Dennis was overoptimistic," she said. "He assumed future generations were bound to learn much more about Etruscan history and thought. But here it is, a century and a half later, and that hasn't happened. The Etruscans remain a mystery. Because we can't decipher their language."

"That's what drew you to them," I said, "their mystery."

"Look, a pair of dice was found in an Etruscan necropolis back in 1848. Dice was a popular game in the ancient world, and it was played like it is today. With the numbers one to six on each die. But these Etruscan dice are inscribed with *words* for the numbers, not numerals. A dozen equally eminent philologists have come up with a dozen different interpretations of those words. And we still don't know which word stands for one or six, or any number in between."

"You'd like to be the one who solves it, or some other part of the mystery. Get your name in the history books. Shared immortality."

Carmen raised her glass and took a long sip. She lowered the glass and turned it slowly on the tablecloth. "It sounds so pretentious, put that way. I can't blame you for mocking."

"I'm not," I told her. "Everybody needs some kind of ambition, just to get up in the morning."

She studied me. "I get a distinct feeling you're *pumping* me, as they say in your business—at least on TV."

I grinned at her. "I'm giving it a clumsy try."

"Why?"

"I'm a snoop by trade. Knowing what makes the people you're dealing with tick sometimes makes it easier to figure out what's going on."

"Aren't you supposed to seduce the girl first?" She had lightened her tone but wasn't quite smiling. "To make sure you get truthful answers?"

"That's what it says in the union rulebook. Trouble is, I tend to forget the questions under those conditions."

She did smile then. "So let me ask you some. Like— what's *your* ambition?"

"To survive the day," I said, "and enjoy it. As long as I'm capable of enjoying."

"I don't get the impression *you* have much trouble with that, the way I read you. You take large-size bites out of life, I think."

"I've broken a few teeth in the attempt."

Carmen laughed. The second cognac was doing its job. Breaking down barriers that shouldn't have been there to begin with. She rested her elbows on the table and her chin on her hands, eyeing me. "Are you married, Peter? You're not, are you?"

"I have been."

"But you've got a girlfriend. Right? Notice, I didn't put that in the plural. Just one—at a time, anyway. A romantic— do I read you right?"

"Last time you analyzed me I was a devil."

"So—a romantic devil. And you're avoiding my implied question. *Have* you got a girlfriend, or are you in the between stage at the moment? My God, that sounds like I'm making a pass . . ." Carmen straightened and finished off her cognac. "Blame it on this."

I smiled at her. "I had the impression you've already got a guy."

She frowned at me. "I don't know why you'd think that . . ." She waited for me to tell her why, but I went on smiling and outwaited her. "It's been a long while since I did," she said finally. "Back in Philly. We were talking marriage, but then I got the offer to go to work for Galton-Stallbrass in New York. At three times what I was earning at the university. So I went, and he wouldn't."

Carmen picked up her empty glass, looked at it, then put it aside. "You're pumping me again."

"Yep."

"Nothing more to tell," she said. "New York turns out to be a downer, for single women past twenty."

"Paris isn't."

"So I've heard. So far I've been too loaded with work to find out if that's really true."

I had an impulse just to kiss her and stop prying. She needed kissing, and I liked her. I hoped she wasn't going to turn out to be responsible for what had happened to Fritz. But I checked the impulse and sank in the next probe.

"What about Yann Bouvier?"

Carmen stared at me, her face darkening. "You think I'm having an affair with him . . ."

"Wrong thought?"

"You have a very mean, relentless side to you."

"Yes."

Carmen sighed. "Oh, hell, I forgive you. You're just doing your job." She shook her head and tried to force a smile, but there was still that heightened color in her cheeks. "You *are* wrong. I like Yann. He *is* the kind of man I could . . . But, he's just not available."

"He's in love with Susan Kape, you mean."

"*Overwhelmed* by her, anyway. I don't mean by her money either. Yann's not like that. But someone as fantastically wealthy as Susan radiates a very potent personal magnetism. *I'm* overwhelmed by it. Look how I tossed away a career at Galton-Stallbrass and came running to work for her."

I kept my tone casual. "Think she'll make you director of her museum?"

Carmen thought about it. Or maybe she was thinking about how she should answer.

"I'm not sure yet," she said finally. "We haven't had a chance to discuss details like that."

"I got the impression," I said, "that your boss wants to be the one who runs the museum. To give herself a reason for living."

Carmen Haung took a long time considering what she wanted to say about that.

She was still taking time when the phone rang.

I picked up the extension the same instant she picked up the phone.

"Miss Haung," a man's voice said in English, "go to the Piazza del Popolo. Walk there. It's a short walk from your hotel. Find a table and wait until one of us contacts you." It wasn't Dollinger's voice. The caller had an Italian accent.

Carmen started to say she would start at once, but the caller had hung up. She crossed the room to put on a flight jacket.

"Meet you in the lobby," I told her. "I forgot my coat in my room." I left quickly while she was picking up her shoulder bag.

Winter in Rome can be more bitter than in Paris, but with mild days and nights in between. This night was one of those. I didn't need the topcoat. Going to my room for it, however, gave me the chance to make a phone call in private. A very short call.

I said three words, hung up, and went down to the Hassler's lobby. With my coat.

⊠ **14** ⊠

CARMEN AND I WAITED WHERE WE'D BEEN INSTRUCTED TO: at a table outside the Bolognese Restaurant, on the Piazza del Popolo. Surrounded by buildings that exhaled the dust of bygone Rome. Not ancient, but old enough. Quattrocento, Cinquecento, Boroque.

Carmen asked the waiter for cognac. That would be her third, and I knew she wasn't normally a big drinker. She was fighting her nerves again. I ordered an *espresso doppio*, and hung the topcoat over the back of my chair, where it wouldn't block the shortest line between my hand and the Hungarian automatic.

The twin churches of Cardinal Gastaldi loomed on our right, and the one where Luther celebrated his last mass was off to our left. Long before that, it was said, Nero was buried across the piazza from our table, at the bottom of the Pincio terraces. But the walnut tree that once marked the spot was gone. Chopped down by an eleventh-century pope after a dream warned him the crows roosting in it were evil spirits.

The only truly ancient thing left wasn't Roman. It was the Egyptian obelisk standing in the center of the vast square, a long way from home. For that obelisk, the emperor who murdered his wife and mother and fiddled while Rome burned was recent history. It was old when Rome was born.

84

It had stood witness to Pharaoh receiving the news that his cavalry had been drowned trying to pursue Moses and his tribe of dissident Jews across the Red Sea.

Now it watched the people milling around the Piazza del Popolo.

So did I, more attentively. I didn't have to pretend I wasn't. Everyone was doing the same. That's what sitting or strolling on the Piazza del Popolo is for. To see and be seen. It was crowded and nobody was moving fast. The cars working through the snarled traffic couldn't, and the strollers jay-walking between the cars didn't want to.

So far I hadn't seen what I was looking for. That was encouraging. If I couldn't spot it, nobody else would.

Our orders arrived. Carmen picked up her cognac, but then scowled and made herself put the glass back down without drinking from it. I sipped my black coffee and looked at the people around us some more.

For a short time I thought what I was looking for might be the two well-dressed men nearby, arguing about something over shopping bags they'd dumped on the table between them. But they got up and left, taking the bags with them. Three middle-aged ladies beat several other groups to the table. I looked elsewhere.

Carmen registered what I was doing, and misinterpreted it. "You think they're already here, checking to make sure we weren't followed?"

"I haven't spotted Dollinger anywhere," I said.

"They could have sent someone else that we wouldn't recognize."

I nodded. I thought I'd already spotted that "someone else" among the crowd strolling round and round the piazza. A scrawny man wearing a shabby suit and an old, wide-brimmed hat. He had passed our table twice, without showing any interest in us. Which wasn't natural. Carmen's combination of gingery-red hair and Oriental face was an attention getter.

She started to reach for her glass again but instead reached past it to touch my hand. "I'm glad you're here with me, Peter."

I looked at her. "Scared?"

"A bit. No, more than a bit. These people we're going to meet tonight—I'd be much *more* frightened if I had to go there alone."

"You knew from the start you were dealing with criminals."

"*Criminals*—we've had this discussion before. I assumed we were dealing with other people like Friedhelm Dollinger. *He* doesn't frighten me. People like him, sure they're jackals, ready to sneak around the corners of some countries' laws. Performing clandestine excavations, smuggling, faking credentials of provenance and transfers of ownership. But without people like that the museums of the world would be half-empty."

"So your jackals are cultural benefactors," I said impatiently. "But now you're afraid of them."

"I didn't expect *killing*," she whispered shakily. "That poor girl at Dollinger's place. I couldn't know something like *that* would happen."

"You think that was your tomb robbers?"

"I just don't know."

"Join the club," I told her. "I don't either. And the police don't."

"But what do you *think*?" Carmen demanded softly but urgently.

"I think you're afraid. But not enough to get up and walk away from it. Right now. You could do that."

I watched her look down at her slim hands, curling them into fists on our table and then forcing them open. "No," she said finally without looking up, "I don't think I *can* do that."

The scrawny man with the wide-brimmed hat was circling

our way again. This time he didn't pretend disinterest. He stopped at our table and leaned toward Carmen.

"Miss Haung, I am the one the man on the phone said would contact you here. You may call me Aldo. You are to come with me, please."

The name he gave didn't mean anything. His English was slow, but the accent wasn't Italian. Dutch perhaps.

Carmen looked at him nervously. "Where is Mr. Dollinger?"

"I don't know about that," Aldo said. "All they told me was to bring you." His voice was thin and mild. No suggestion of menace in it. Nor in what I could see of his wrinkled face. The upper part of it was shadowed by his hat brim. He made a small gesture at me. "This man is your bodyguard?"

"Yes," Carmen told him, getting to her feet. "He comes with me."

"All right. They told me that. *Come*."

"Wait a minute," I snapped, "I've got to pay the bill here first."

Carmen and Aldo waited impatiently while I made a production of examining the bill and counting out the proper amount of money. Then I stood up and turned from them to take my coat off the chair. I picked it up by the collar and turned back, swinging it around with a flourish to hang it over my left shoulder. The coattails just missed Aldo's face and knocked the hat off his head.

He gaped at me, startled. I began apologizing profusely for my clumsiness.

His thinning hair was white, and so were his straight eyebrows. His eyes could have been green or blue.

He bent down to retrieve his hat from the ground. I bent at the same time and beat him to it, straightening with it in my hand.

Aldo straightened and said, "Give me my hat, please."

I continued to hold it while I apologized to him again. He

yanked the hat from my hand and set it back on his head, shadowing his face again. Then he led us off across the big piazza.

I hoped my play with the hat had accomplished its purpose. But I didn't look back to check it out.

Aldo left the Piazza del Popolo behind and walked us three blocks along the Via Flaminia. Parked there was an old Volkswagen. A battered beetle, recently repainted black. It had a Naples license plate. I memorized the number, though I doubted that it would be any help.

Aldo opened the Volkswagen's doors. I motioned Carmen into the backseat and got in front with Aldo. He drove off with us. He stuck with Via Flaminia all the way to the Ponte Milvio, the bridge where Constantine paused in his attack on Rome to swear to God that if he conquered it he would make Christianity the empire's official religion. He won and kept his word. Christians stopped being persecuted and could devote themselves to persecuting the other religions.

Aldo looked in his rearview mirror as he drove over the Tiber. He'd done that several times before. There hadn't been anybody following us then, and there wasn't now. The small piazza on the other end of the bridge, a busy open market by day, was deserted now except for a few parked vehicles. Two cars and a Fiat van. I glimpsed a shadowy figure behind the wheel of the van as we rode past it.

We turned into a narrow street, turned at the next corner, and again at the next. Slowing, Aldo drove us back into the little piazza and parked. The figure I'd glimpsed got down out of the van. A big man wearing a lumber jacket, dungarees, and work boots. He gave Aldo an all-clear signal, final assurance we hadn't been tailed.

"We get out here," Aldo told us as he opened his door to do so. I climbed out on my side and helped Carmen extricate herself from the cramped backseat. By then I had the van's license memorized. This one was from Ravenna.

The big man from the van came to meet us. He was an inch or two below my height, with a torso like a wine cask and fair, curly hair. About thirty-five years old. His face was round as a full moon, with a lot of padding under the tight, weathered skin. Solid padding; no jiggle to it when he moved.

He offered Carmen a jumbo-sized hand and a smile. It was a hearty fat-man smile, but I didn't think much of his size was fat. "Welcome, Miss Haung," he said as she allowed her small hand to be engulfed in his. "My name's Robby. You're right on time."

His voice was the one on the phone. He *was* Italian, but he'd spent a good deal of time in the States. Sounded like New York. His tone was as amiable as his smile, but he looked to me like a man who could stop being that way very suddenly.

"I expected Dollinger to be here," Carmen told him uneasily.

"He's busy elsewhere right now," Robby said. "I'm in charge from here on. Don't worry, you're in good hands with me."

I hoped that didn't mean we wouldn't meet Dollinger that night. That was the main reason I'd come. I wanted to have a talk with him, almost as much as I wanted one with Arnaud Galice. I wasn't as eager to meet the spooky lady that night, even with what was holstered to my belt. Not without some backup. Preferably a platoon.

Robby released Carmen's hand and turned his amiable fat-man smile on me. "The bodyguard, eh? I'll have to frisk you."

Definitely New York.

"Not necessary," I told him. "I *am* carrying."

"You'll have to get rid of it. I don't want any guns along. Chuck it in the river, or—"

"No," I said flatly. "I'm being paid to do a job. The job's protecting Miss Haung. I can't do that with my fingernails."

"Suit yourself," Robby said carelessly. "You get rid of the gun or you stay behind."

"If he does," Carmen said quickly, "I do, too. I'm not going anywhere without him."

Robby turned his head and took a slow look at her. "Susan Kape won't like you if you queer our deal."

"*She's* the one who hired him. To make sure I'm safe."

He looked a little insulted. "You're safe with me."

I kept my own tone friendly. "Don't be a hard-nose, Robby. You want to kiss all that money good-bye just to prove you're the boss?"

He went on looking at Carmen. She had difficulty continuing to meet his stare, though there was no threat in it. But she managed to. Finally he said, "What the hell, it doesn't matter. Ain't gonna be any trouble, anyway. We want the same thing, right?"

"I hope so," Carmen said in a strained voice.

He had his smile back in full operation when he turned to me again. "So *carry* your toy if it makes you feel better. You won't need it for anything more than that."

"Good," I said. "Then I'll earn my pay without having to work too hard."

"That's the best way." He opened the back of the van and motioned us in.

Aldo climbed in first. I boosted Carmen up and got inside after her. The floor inside the van was padded with several layers of old carpeting. As we settled down on it Robby shut the door on us. But he didn't lock it.

We sat there in the dark. The back of the van had a window, but it had been painted black. We couldn't look out and no light came in.

Robby started the van. It made a turn in the little piazza and headed away from the Tiber. It executed more turns, and my sense of direction got lost. After that all I could do was listen to the traffic outside the van. There got to be a lot of it after a while. And then less and less. And then none at all.

I checked the luminous hands of my watch from time to time.

Wherever the van was carrying us, it took almost two hours.

⊠ **15** ⊠

I OPENED THE VAN'S REAR DOOR AND GOT OUT, LOOKING around as Carmen and Aldo came out after me. Clouds scudded across the night sky but didn't blank out all the moon and starlight. After the total dark inside the van, that was enough to show me the terrain we were in.

I discovered there wasn't much to see. We were in the bottom of a wide ravine. Its sides rose some twenty feet and blocked the view on either side.

The side to my left was a slope overgrown with wild bushes and topped by stunted, leafless trees. The side to my right had been a slope, too, but sometime in the past few years the earth forming that slope had slid into the bottom of the ravine, leaving behind a low cliff of bared stone.

The van had stopped because it couldn't go any farther. The way ahead was blocked by a looming mound of frozen mud with dead branches and chunks of rock sticking out of it. I did a quick scan of the sky. Orion's position told me the ravine angled ahead in an approximately northwest direction. Looking behind me, I made out a pointy hill with a pair of branchless trees on its summit. I put that together with the fact that we were within two hours' drive of Rome, probably but not certainly north of it.

Splendid. With that much information about where we

were, twenty search parties aided by several helicopters could comb central Italy for a thousand years and not find it.

It was colder in the ravine than the streets of Rome. I put on my topcoat but left it unbuttoned as I squinted through the night shadows at one other thing I'd seen. It was a Land Rover, parked with no lights close to the cliff side of the ravine.

There was someone standing between it and the cliff, looking at us over its roof. The head was high enough for the figure to be a man or a tall woman. It was too dark there to guess which.

Robby had come around from the front of the van, carrying two long flashlights. One was lit, its beam aimed down at our feet. He handed the other to Aldo and told Carmen, "Stick close behind me, Miss Haung, and watch the ground so you don't trip over anything."

He began climbing up over the mound, picking his way between obstacles projecting out of it. I followed him, with Carmen holding tight to my left arm.

Aldo brought up the rear, switching on his flashlight to illuminate the ground just ahead of us. I looked back when we reached the top of the mound.

The vague, silent figure was still there, motionless behind the Land Rover. I thought I caught a glint of a rifle or shotgun barrel on its roof. But that could have been nerves playing tricks on my night vision.

We tailed Robby down the other side of the mound. Beyond it the ravine became narrower and densely wooded. Robby led the way through a path broken through tangles of underbrush and vines. After some thirty feet the path diverged to the right. It ended at the base of the cliff. Robby shoved aside a tall, thorny bush, revealing a dark opening behind it.

It was a man-made opening, cut neatly into the cliff base. About six and a half feet high. Four feet wide at the bottom, but tapering at the top. Robby's flashlight shone inside it, revealing a passage, as high and wide as the entrance, leading straight into the heart of the living rock.

"This is it," he told us, like an MC announcing his big act of the evening. "Covered for a couple thousand years by a landslide from farther up. That's what hid it all this time."

"And saved what's inside," Aldo put in, his tone almost reverent.

"Yeah," the big man who called himself Robby said, "until last spring. Heavy rains started a big mudslide down here that opened it up. But nobody comes around here. It still wouldn't have been found except for a guy out hunting small game. His dog spotted the hole and went in. This hunter went in after it, and told what he found to a friend of mine."

"Let's go *in*," Carmen said. I could sense an unstable mixture in her: impatience and a bad case of the jitters.

I turned abruptly to my left, peering at a shadowed space between a scrub tree and a boulder. One of the darker shadows seemed to be a figure standing there. But it didn't move, and I couldn't be as sure of it as I was of the one by the Land Rover.

This gang having some silent guards outside in the ravine didn't worry me much. They had nothing to gain by harming Susan Kape's emissaries. But I did wonder if one of the vague figures could be Arnaud Galice—or the woman assassin.

Aldo pushed at me lightly. "Go *ahead*, what are you waiting for?"

Carmen had already vanished inside the passage with Robby. I went in after them, with Aldo at my heels. The two flashlights illuminated the passage. Its walls and curved roof had been chiseled smooth, and there were traces of paint on them. The stone floor was covered by a thick layer of caked mud, slightly springy underfoot.

The passage grew wider. Robby stopped and said, "Wait here a minute. I want to light up the chambers before you see them."

He disappeared into the deeper murk of the passage, leaving Aldo behind with Carmen and me.

"How many chambers are there?" I asked Aldo. Sometimes these passages linked dozens of them.

"Only two," he said, "but richer than any entire necropolis discovered in this century." Aldo shone his light on the passage wall to our right. "Look what stands guard over this sepulcher."

A winged demon was carved into the smoothed wall there, in bas-relief. The body and bearded face were those of a man, but the mouth had a beastlike snarl that bared sharp tusks, and the ears were double normal size, their tops pointed. One hand held a big hammer upraised threateningly, and the other grasped a fanged serpent.

"The Etruscan version of Charon," Carmen said softly, studying it with intense interest.

"Almost certainly," Aldo agreed, "judging by the hammer. Although sometimes Charon carries an oar or a torch instead."

Aldo was apparently the gang's equivalent of Carmen Haung: their antiquities expert.

Carmen placed both palms against the stone figure, leaning against it, her eyes closing for a few moments. Watching her, Aldo nodded understandingly. "Yes, one reaches across most of recorded history to touch it. You feel that, too."

She looked a bit dazed for a second after opening her eyes. She dropped her hands, not responding to Aldo.

Robby's hulking figure reappeared. "Okay," he told us cheerfully, "it's all set for you." He sounded more than ever like a showman proudly presenting his star attraction.

He led the way. Some twenty feet deeper, yellowish light poured out of a masonry doorway to the first burial vault. We stepped through it and were surrounded by a blaze of colors.

We were in a large, square, damp-aired chamber. The

only things in it that didn't look like they'd been there since centuries before Christ were the large kerosene lamps that Robby had lit, their gleam reflecting off all the colors.

Above us, beams, rafters, and fan-patterned moldings had been carved out of the living rock, and painted in imitation of the ceiling of a room in a wood-built house. The colors radiating from there—and from the frescos painted on the walls—were predominantly strong yellows, reds, and blues. Other colors glinted from the multitude of objects crowding the chamber.

Angled out from the walls were four stone ledges: the biers on which the dead were laid. Indicating that this tomb was from an archaic period of Etruscan history, before they began adopting the Roman custom of enclosing their dead inside stone sarcophagi.

Of the bodies that had been stretched out on these stone platforms, and the clothes they'd worn, nothing was left. Not even their dust or fragments of bones. But the wealth of necklaces, rings, bracelets, brooches, earrings, and other durable ornaments they'd worn, lay there in the positions they'd occupied on the corpses.

Between the stone biers were tables and tripods of rust-eroded iron. They were arrayed with exquisitely decorated objects of gold and silver, bronze and earthenware, glass and alabaster. Dishes and goblets, ornamented mirrors and boxes opened to show the jewelry inside, figured perfume bottles and unguent jars, sculptured candelabra, elegant vases and pitchers.

Dominating the center of the burial chamber was the full-sized upper figure of a woman in bronze, resting on a sculptured marble pedestal. Around it were ranged rows of large amphoras and bronze figurines whose heads came up to the level of my hips. The elongated style of these figurines gave another indication this tomb belonged to a period before Roman influence set in. So did the decoration of the amphoras:

the figures painted black on the reddish yellow of the baked clay.

Susan Kape—or the photos Dollinger had shown her—had exaggerated. Nothing was in "mint condition." Everything had suffered in some degree from the attack of time. But most of the damage to various objects could be eradicated with modern techniques, like the benzol and morpholine baths used to remove discolorations from ancient gold objects.

Much worse—irreparable—was the damage time had inflicted on the frescos around the walls. Moisture had seeped into the stucco base on which they had been painted. Most of it had fallen away from the stone walls, crumbling to mud. It was impossible to guess what the scenes on these walls had once been, though the fragments left were surprisingly vivid. Here a dove in flight . . . there a rabbit hopping through tall grass . . . in another spot the foliage of a palm. But I doubted that even those fragments could ever be detached without disintegrating.

That left, however, more than enough that *could* be plundered—from that first burial chamber alone—to make any museum or private collector drool with greed.

What wasn't there was the man I'd hoped to find waiting for us: Friedhelm Dollinger. I remarked on that to the big man with the fat smile.

"I told you," Robby said offhandedly, "he's busy elsewhere."

Carmen didn't like it either. "I thought that meant *here*." She was studying Robby with a troubled frown. "He was *supposed* to be."

Robby spread his hands and looked helpless. "Well, he ain't."

I said, "So where is he?"

"Danmed if I know. Anyway, Miss Haung, what's it matter? Dollinger's just our go-between, not any kind of expert on Etruscan stuff. That's *your* department, making sure all of this is genuine. You need any help checking any of it, Aldo can handle whatever you want to know."

"Be pleased to, Miss Haung," Aldo told her with a small smile that was either sly or superior, or both.

"Thank you," she said stiffly, "but I'm capable of handling this myself. And I prefer to."

She went first to take a close look at the fragments of wall painting that remained. Those, I'd noted, had attracted her most from the moment we'd entered the vault. Her eyes gleamed with excitement as she studied the first fragment, the one with the dove. Reaching out, she touched its surface at one edge very lightly.

"Careful," Robby warned her. "What's left of these frescos is barely hanging on. No way to get any of it off intact. We tried."

Paying no attention to him, Carmen moved on eagerly to the next fragments. I watched her finally turn away from them, with obvious reluctance, to examine the multitude of objects displayed between the biers. She took a powerful magnifying glass from her shoulder bag and used it for a closer study of several pieces. I registered the way Robby and Aldo watched her do so. They were relaxed, unworried.

I drifted close to the effigy of the woman on the marble pedestal. She was fashioned out of separate sheets of bronze, nailed together after the sculptor had hammered each sheet into the contours desired. The finishing touches had been added with delicate chisel work. This was the kind of craftsmanship that even the ancient Greeks conceded the Etruscans did better than anyone else.

Aldo came up beside me. "Superb work, eh?"

"Superb," I agreed.

"Priceless."

The bronze woman's hair was meticulously braided, hanging over one shoulder and down between her full breasts. In one half-raised hand she held an inkwell, in the other a stylus. Her eyes stared at me unwaveringly.

"The goddess of Fate," Aldo murmured. "See what she holds in her hands. To mark down her final decision on the destiny of each of us."

The other chamber of the sepulcher was stranger.

◪ **16** ◪

THERE WERE NO PLAIN, SEPARATE BIERS IN THE SECOND chamber. Instead there was a large, paw-footed double couch, sculpted out of white marble. The counterpane and piled cushions on it were of the same marble, given a softness by the sculptor's art. At the foot of the couch, and on both sides of it, were tables covered with objects as precious as those in the first chamber.

All of this was reproduced in the gaily colored wall painting behind the couch. With one striking difference. In the fresco, the paw-footed couch was occupied by a man and a woman.

Around the other three walls the frescos had been almost obliterated by the same moisture that had ruined the ones in the other room. Only small fragments were left. The wall painting behind the marble couch had suffered extensive damage, too. But a large central portion remained almost intact.

It was a banquet scene, with dancing musicians around its crumbling edges. The couple formed its focal point, each half reclining on the festive couch with the left elbow resting on raised cushions. In her right hand the woman held out an egg to the man. He was offering her a goblet of wine.

Their faces were turned toward each other, exchanging a joyful, confident smile.

The jewelry they wore in the picture lay now on the burial chamber's marble couch, where their bodies had long ago disintegrated into nothingness. But in the fresco they continued to be vividly alive.

Carmen stood in front of the painting, entranced. I didn't blame her.

The woman had the stylized Etruscan beauty: her skin painted white, her eyes long and almond-shaped, her nose forming an almost straight line with her forehead. The tunic she wore was purple, signifying nobility.

The man was naked to the waist, his purple toga gathered around his hips. His skin was colored the customary dark red, and he had the conventional round eyes. He wore a short beard, and a golden garland on his head. A round shield, with two battling lions on it, leaned against the painted couch by him, probably meaning he'd been a military officer.

"The way they're smiling at each other," Carmen murmured dreamily. "One last smile—the one they took with them into death. Into another life, they thought. Or hoped."

"That smile's lasted over two thousand years so far," I said. "That's not bad. Most marriages don't last that long."

She shot me an irritated look, then forced herself to turn away from the picture and begin the job of examining the treasures in the chamber. She started with the jewelry the smiling couple had left behind on the big marble couch.

There was a good deal of it, but the most valuable single item was a crescent-shaped pectoral the woman in the fresco was pictured wearing over her bosom. It was made from a single thin, flexible sheet of gold, embossed with rows of tiny figures: winged horses, palms, and griffons. There was a pectoral like this one in the Vatican's Museo Gregoriano Etrusco and another in New York's Metropolitan. Either of those would fetch millions in today's art-as-investment market.

How *many* millions would depend on auction-house hype and the competitive frenzy of hedge-against-inflation bidders. One thing was axiomatic: the price, for objets d'art with this much historical glamor, multiplied astronomically each time they came up for sale.

Carmen prowled the room inspecting other individual items, occasionally devoting closer scrutiny to one of them as she had in the first chamber. Robby and Aldo watched her without anxiety. Now and then one of them glanced my way, taking in my expression as I watched her. Mostly I looked bored. And did some confined prowling of my own to relieve the waiting for Carmen to render her verdict.

Robby began checking the time on his watch. At last he said, "Well, Miss Haung, satisfied?"

"I haven't examined all of it yet," she said.

"You've seen *enough*, for Christ's sake."

I looked at him. "What's your hurry, Robby?"

"I want to drop you two back in Rome while it's still night," he explained. "Be reasonable, Miss Haung. You haven't seen anything that looks phony to you, right? We wouldn't have brought you here if you were likely to. You know it's all genuine by now. You can report that to Susan Kape."

Carmen turned to gaze again at the smiling couple in the fresco. After a moment she said, "That could probably be removed, with proper care."

"Sure," Robby said, "by a team of experts, taking weeks or months to do the job. That's too much time for us. We're gonna take what we can move out fast. Which'll come to more than enough to be worth the price."

Carmen turned away from the wall painting, looking at him thoughtfully. "Everything I've examined does *look* authentic," she admitted. There was still a hint of that jittery undertone in her voice. "But I want to take along one piece for testing. To make sure."

That creased a frown into his beefy face. "You already tested those two pieces Dollinger let you have."

"But without proof they came from *here*."

Robby considered it for a few moments more before dropping the frown. "Why not . . ." He picked up a little alabaster cosmetics box from one of the crowded tables. "How about this?"

Carmen shook her head. "No, *I* want to choose what I take."

Robby hesitated, then put down the box and told her, "Okay, but make it something small enough so you can carry it out of the country with no risk." He smiled again. "And that ain't worth *too* much."

What Carmen selected was smaller than the palm of her hand: a terra-cotta figurine of a squatting monkey. I watched her place it carefully inside her shoulder bag. It was one of the least valuable pieces in this sepulcher, but a perfect choice for the purpose of scientific testing. Clay objects are among the easiest to date accurately.

There was a little item of the same sort tucked deep inside the left-hand pocket of my coat. I'd filched it off a table full of them during a moment when neither Aldo nor Robby was looking my way. They hadn't noticed it was gone so far, and I hoped neither was going to before we were clear of them.

⊠ **17** ⊠

My appointment with Major Diego Bandini was for 8 a.m. the following morning. I left the Hassler at 7:30. A cold, steady drizzle was falling out of a low, gloomy sky. Half a dozen hotel guests were crowded under the hotel canopy outside, waiting impatiently for the doorman to somehow conjure a taxi out of the drizzle. Impossible. Along every street around there, Romans with early jobs to get to would be grabbing any free taxi that did make a magical appearance long before it could reach the Hassler.

I put on my corduroy cap and walked it, along Via Sistina and cutting over into Via Ludovisi. I reached the Via Veneto fifteen wet minutes from the hotel and ducked into Doney's Café. Doney's was Diego's favorite place for early morning and late evening social meetings. He and his wife—a Dutch actress who did commercials for Italian TV—lived only a few blocks away, on Via Pinciana facing the Villa Borghese park.

I whipped off my cap, spattering water on a floor already slick from so many other customers doing the same. The bar was crowded. Diego wasn't part of the crowd yet. I paid the cashier for my ticket, picked up a sweet roll, and shouted for a double espresso over a number of shoulders.

The service was fast. It had to be. Most Roman males shave getting to work on time very close, and they need that

104

last caffeine jolt in a hurry to shock them fully awake. I did, too, that morning. Another night with too little sleep and it was beginning to take its inevitable toll.

It had been past 2:30 A.M. when Robby and Aldo dropped us off a couple blocks behind the Hassler Hotel. Half an hour more before I hit my bed. When the alarm got me up I mercifully refrained from calling and waking Carmen Haung. Instead I'd left her a note before going out of the hotel. It said I couldn't make the 11 A.M flight back to Paris, booked the previous day. If she wanted to wait, I expected to be ready to go by late afternoon or evening.

There was no place left in Doney's to sit down. I leaned against a marble pillar and made fast work of my coffee and roll. It helped. I was setting the empty cup on a shelf when Diego Bandini came in out of the drizzle. He wasn't at all wet. He would have driven his car over and parked right outside the entrance in the strictly enforced no-parking zone. Cops get special privileges everywhere in the world. Getting along without them had required a sobering adjustment period after I'd gone private.

Diego looked dashing in his resplendent *carabinieri* major's uniform. All Italian uniforms are calculated to make any male look dashing. But for years he'd been the despair of Roman matchmakers because of unexplainable seizures of painful bashfulness in the presence of any pretty woman. Until the one from Holland came along, ignored his stuttered excuses, dragged him off, bedded him, and married him.

Diego called for an espresso and got served even faster than I had. He brought it over to the pillar beside me. "Have you checked on Fritz yet this morning?" He always spoke with me in French. His English was rudimentary, and while I could handle an ordinary conversation in Italian, it had to be so slow it drove him mad.

"I phoned the hospital before leaving the hotel this morning," I told Diego. "The floor nurse said Fritz should be well enough to start taking phone calls himself by this evening.''

"That's good news. Once whoever tried to kill him learns that, they won't have any motive for trying again. It will be obvious that if he's that well he'll have already told others whatever it is they didn't want him to.''

I agreed and asked, "Did your people get anything worth the effort?''

Diego finished off his espresso and fished three small photographs from his pocket. "That was good work, getting his hat off.''

I looked at the top picture and saw what had worried me last evening. With his hat shadowing his face, Aldo could have been Frank Sinatra for all anyone could see of it. The other two were perfect. A clear profile of Aldo gaping at me after his hat was knocked off. A full-face shot when I'd picked it up and he was demanding it back.

"Who took these,'' I asked Diego, "the nice middle-aged ladies at the table near us?''

"One of them. The other two were just friends she brought along with her for cover. You can keep these copies; we have others. I'll start having them checked against our rogues' gallery this morning. But it could take a long time, you realize, unless you can narrow it down. You told me you suspected that whoever picked you up last night would be connected to a gang in a criminal operation. We have so *many* criminals in our files. What *kind* would help.''

"*Tombaroli,*'' I told him. It was the name Italian police applied to their tomb robbers.

"Ah. That does narrow the field considerably.''

"This one,'' I said, flicking the photos he'd given me, "knows a lot about the Etruscans.''

"That narrows our search even more,'' Diego said, "I don't suppose you know his name.''

"Aldo, he said, but I think he's as Dutch as your wife.''

"That may be useful, too. This gang he is part of—it has already robbed a tomb? Or it's still in the planning stage?"

"They're going to any moment. Perhaps tonight."

"Where?"

"I don't know," I told Diego. "Except it's within two hours of Rome. That's the maximum distance. Could be closer, if we were driven around in circles for a while." I described the ride in the blacked-out back of the van and told Diego what little I knew about Robby.

The name and description didn't ring a bell for Diego. "Robby—is that his first or last name?"

"Could be either, but probably neither." I pocketed the pictures of Aldo and took out a slip of paper on which I'd jotted the license numbers of the van and the black Volkswagen. "This probably won't lead to anything either."

Diego glanced at the numbers. "Ravenna and Naples. And the tomb would be in Tuscany. Three different areas. Well, we'll check them."

"There's a shady art dealer named Friedhelm Dollinger," I told him. "He's acting as intermediary for this gang, and he should be somewhere in Italy at this point. You're bound to have a dossier on him. He's operated in Italy before. If you can locate him, it could lead to the rest of them."

Diego took out a slim gold pen and printed Dollinger's name under the license numbers as I spelled it out for him. "I'll spread the word to all *carabinieri* posts. There is a small government reward, as well as almost certain promotion, for anyone who catches a *tombaroli* band in operation. That should make everyone eager to cooperate."

"Except for the ones getting paid by the *tombaroli* to look the other way."

"I am forced to admit, not every Italian policeman is as totally honest as I am."

"Not many of them have a wife bringing in a small fortune from television commercials."

Diego smiled. "I think of her as my good fairy. A certain

amount of prosperity is sometimes more compelling than a
noble conscience.'' He put the slip of paper in his pocket.
''Where will I be able to get in touch with you?''

''I'll be at the Hassler until some time this afternoon.
After that, call my place in Paris. Leave a message if I'm
out.''

''Be sure to give Fritz my warmest affection,'' Diego said
as we walked together toward Doney's entrance. He came to
a pensive halt when we reached it, ignoring the fact that we
were blocking the way for everyone else trying to get in or
out. Everybody who was blocked looked at his uniform and
refrained from complaining about it.

''I assume this *tombaroli* plunder is intended for France,''
Diego said, eyeing me gravely. ''Would you be able to tell
me *who* they intend to deliver it to?''

''No, I'm afraid I can't, Diego.''

''I was afraid of that, too,'' Diego said, with a certain
amount of restrained humor. We stepped out into the drizzle,
allowing other customers to use Doney's entrance once more.

I had a second breakfast at Café Greco on the Via Con-
dotti. Food calories can substitute for sufficient sleep in sup-
plying energy, in short spurts. It gets shorter as you pile up
those white nights.

This time I ordered a mozzarella and prosciutto sandwich
from the front counter, together with a tall orange juice.
Leaving it to the waiter to find me, I wandered back through
the aging charms of the small, cozy rooms until I spotted
Francesco Ascoli.

He was relaxed in a moth-eaten red plush sofa under a
painting of Byron—one of the many illustrious names who'd
patronized the Café Greco over a couple centuries. On the
little round marble table in front of Ascoli was a cappuccino,
into which he was dumping three cubes of sugar when I
arrived. He was a small, nattily dressed, fox-faced man in

his midthirties, with an entirely bald pate that was freckled in all seasons.

Ascoli had been the third person I'd called in Rome from the phone at the Select in Montparnasse. He was a specialist in testing antiquities for the government commission devoted to recovering stolen works of art. I'd only met him once before, through Fritz. Fleetingly I wondered how I'd ever get along without the vast network of contacts Fritz had built up over so many years.

I made myself stop thinking along that line as I shook Ascoli's hand and sat down beside him. The waiter found me in that same moment. As he set my sandwich and juice on the table Ascoli took a swallow of his cappuccino, looked pleased with the taste, and asked me in meticulous French, "Now what can I do for you, Monsieur Sawyer? I've only a few minutes before I must return to my work."

"It's actually for Fritz Donhoff," I made a point of telling him. "Fritz would have come himself, but he's been hurt and is in a Paris hospital at present."

"Oh, I am extremely sad to hear that," Ascoli said and sounded like he meant it. "Is it very serious?"

"It was, but he's on his way to recovery now."

"Thank the Lord for that."

"Yes." I gently took what I'd lifted at the tomb out of my pocket. I'd wrapped it in a small towel that used to belong to the Hassler Hotel. I put it on our table and opened the towel. "Fritz wants to know if you can make whatever tests are necessary on this, as soon as possible."

It was, like the piece Carmen had chosen, a little terra-cotta figurine. This one was of a kneeling woman. Ascoli picked it up, handling it with less trepidation than I had, and peered at it lying in the palm of his hand. After a moment he turned it over and looked at the back, then held it between thumb and forefinger to see its base.

"What is it?" he asked.

"It's supposed to be Etruscan."

"Well, it could be, of course. But you have reason to suspect it may be a copy?"

"We want to be certain, one way or the other."

Ascoli put the figurine back down on the towel and took another big gulp from his cup. "Easy enough to find out. I can take care of that for you as soon as I have time. At the moment I'm quite overloaded with work."

"Fritz asked me to tell you he would appreciate it *enormously* if you could make the tests on this piece today," I said. "And that I should pay you whatever you think fair for your troubles. In cash, of course. Nothing recorded for the income tax snoopers to poke their noses into."

"Hmmm . . ." Ascoli emptied his cup. "Some time this afternoon?"

"That would be fine." I wrote the Hassler's phone number, and the number of my room, on a slip of paper from my notebook and gave it to him.

He rewrapped the figurine in the hotel towel and marched out with it. I ate my sandwich, drank my orange juice, paid the bill for both of us, and walked back through the continuing drizzle to the Hassler.

Carmen Haung was gone, leaving a note. It explained she *had* to catch the eleven o'clock plane. Susan Kape already had her friend at the Louvre standing by, waiting to take her monkey figurine in for testing that afternoon. Because of the rain and traffic, Carmen's note pointed out, she'd thought it wisest to start off early and make sure she didn't miss her flight. She hoped I didn't mind.

I didn't. It wasn't company I needed at that point. Going up to my room with its beautiful view of Rome in the rain, I took a hot bath, climbed into bed, and settled into a blissful nap.

It lasted four hours before I was awakened by the phone call from Francesco Ascoli.

⊠ **18** ⊠

"IF IT *WAS* ARNAUD GALICE," FRITZ TOLD ME, "HE'S changed himself beyond recognition. The same height, but nothing else the same. As you'll remember, he was quite stout."

"As stout as you, when you're healthy."

Fritz went on as though I hadn't spoken. "And with chunky features. This man I saw is slim, with a thin nose and lean cheeks. If it *was* Galice, he's been through a strenuous diet and had a face job. Also, this man has a short, pointy beard and full head of hair, both black. Whereas Arnaud Galice was balding and clean-shaven, and the little hair he had was fair."

"Yet you did recognize him."

"*Recognize* is too definite a word for it. This man *reminded* me of Galice. The way he *walked.* Galice fell from a porch roof and injured his spine when he was about ten. It left him with this peculiar gait—throwing his right foot out to the side with each step, and alternately hitching his left hip forward. Not enough to be called a limp. You wouldn't notice it unless you were looking for it or had observed him over a long time."

I couldn't remember noticing it. But I'd only seen Arnaud Galice twice. On both occasions he'd been sitting most of

the time. Fritz had known him, through his father, since he'd
been a kid.

"Let me have it from the top," I said. "When and where
you first saw this man who may or may not be Arnaud Galice."

I hadn't had a chance to see Fritz the previous evening.
After my second meeting with Francesco Ascoli there'd been
another with Major Diego Bandini, who reported that they
hadn't found Aldo or Robby among their rogues' gallery files
as yet, and that all *carabinieri* posts had been alerted to look
for Dollinger. The license numbers I'd memorized belonged,
as I'd figured, to stolen vehicles.

When I'd been ready to leave Rome, the only flight I could
get on landed me in Paris at midnight. By which time Fritz
was sleeping under sedatives and not to be disturbed.

This morning Paris was cold but clear. The sunlight
streaming into Fritz's hospital room showed him to be back
among the living, with the head of his bed cranked up to
prop him in a half-sitting position. His hospital gown bulged
with the thick bandaging across his chest and midsection, his
face and hands still had a wasted look, and his voice was
draggy. But he'd definitely won his battle with Death. This
time.

That's the trouble with that kind of fight. You can win a
hundred of them and it doesn't change the fact that you're
going to lose the war in the end. But if you relished bucking
the odds as much as Fritz, holding off that end had a kick of
its own.

"I wasn't making any progress in discovering who Friedhelm Dollinger has been associating with lately," Fritz told
me. "So on Friday afternoon I decided to stake out his place
for a time. To see if I could spot anything of interest going
on there. I was in a taxi, on my way there, when I first saw
the lean man I've described. On the Quai de Montebello. He
was two blocks from Dollinger's building, walking away from
his block and turning up Rue des Bernadins."

"And the way he walked reminded you of Arnaud Galice."

"Strongly. I paid the taxi and got out as quickly as I could. But by the time I entered the Rue des Bernadins the man I'd seen had disappeared. I spent the rest of that day asking my contacts to make inquiries about Galice. And that night I went back to the Quai de Montebello. There is a bistro on the corner of Dollinger's block, with a glass-enclosed terrace projecting onto the pavement."

"I've seen it," I said.

"I sat in there from nine until they closed at eleven. The man I thought might be Galice didn't show up. I tried it again at intervals the next day, Saturday, taking a final stroll down there shortly before midnight."

I glowered at Fritz. "In the rain. At your age. When are you going to learn to take better care of yourself?"

He smiled at me. "It's sometimes tempting to see what you can still get away with, at my age."

I found myself remembering the goddess of Fate in the Estruscan burial vault. She'd apparently decided it wasn't time to write finis to Fritz yet, by rain or bullets.

"I was just turning the corner into the Quai de Montebello," Fritz resumed, "when I saw my man getting out of a cab in front of Dollinger's building. He punched the combination to unlock the door there and went in. I waited in a dark doorway. Not for long. He came out in less than five minutes and walked away quickly, turning into the first street leading away from the Seine."

"Toward Place Maubert."

"Yes. I followed. When I turned the corner, I saw he had stopped to look at the display window of a boutique."

"And he saw you."

"I was in shadow," Fritz told me, "and I turned immediately into the nearest doorway. He couldn't have made out my face. Only my general build, with nothing to distinguish me from other men of that same build."

"Unless *you* were a problem he was already worrying about," I said. "Because Dollinger had just told him Susan Kape had hired you."

"Obvious, in hindsight. And that would mean, of course, that someone who knew about it told Dollinger."

I was fairly sure who that someone was by then. I thought about it as Fritz told me how his Saturday night in the rain had ended.

"When I peeked out of the doorway, he was walking off again. By then I was almost certain it was Arnaud Galice. I tailed him across Place Maubert, into the Rue de la Montagne Sainte Geneviève. Where he turned into a building entrance. And then stepped out with a gun and shot at me. And that's all I remember until I woke up here."

"I guess you've told all this to Gojon by now," I said.

"Most of it, last evening. Not about what Susan Kape has gotten herself involved with. But the rest, yes."

"Including about Galice."

"The commissaire told me you already asked him to check on Galice. He hasn't turned up anything on him as yet." ·

"*I* found out something about his death," I told Fritz. There'd been a message on my machine when I'd gotten in last night, from one of my Intelligence contacts. I'd phoned him before coming to the hospital this morning. "Galice was found drowned in a little harbor near Istanbul two years back. His face was too bloated from immersion by the time they fished him out to recognize it. The police identified him by his name inscribed on the wallet in his pocket and also on the gold watch he was still wearing."

"I have a bit more than that," Fritz informed me, somewhat smug about it. "After Commissaire Gojon left last evening I had a call. From Mimi Nogaret, who asks that I give you her love. She seems to find you attractive. A touch of senility, perhaps."

"What's she got?"

"According to her information, before his interesting demise Arnaud Galice got himself in trouble with some Turkish heroin exporters. Seems he was down to driving a T.I.R. truck for them between Istanbul and Munich. With large hidden compartments in it for carrying their heroin. But he failed to arrive in Munich on his last trip. The truck was found, but not Galice or the heroin. The Turks assumed he sold it himself elsewhere, and used the considerable amount of money he would have gotten for that shipment to help him do a vanishing act. They are not the kind to forgive and forget."

"Or to stop looking for him," I said. "Unless they thought he was dead."

"Precisely. So, a number of possibilities. They found him and drowned him. Or he went back to Istanbul and someone else killed him. Or he committed suicide . . ."

"Or he put his watch and wallet on someone else and drowned him. To take the heat off. And he's still alive."

"I think so." Fritz put a hand to his bandaged chest and forced a slight smile.

"With a logical motive for shooting you," I said. "Not to stop you from investigating Dollinger. Galice was just scared you recognized him and would spread the word. Then he'd have the Turks hunting for him again."

"I assume that was his reason," Fritz agreed with a trace of growing fatigue. "But he never was a good shot."

"Thank God for small favors." I stood up, ready to leave and let him get some more sleep.

"By the way," Fritz told me, "Commissaire Gojon came up with a nugget of information along with his questions last evening."

I stopped, looking down at him. "About what?"

"His investigators have discovered a number of long-distance calls recorded over the past couple weeks between Friedhelm Dollinger's apartment and a number in Venice. The commissaire requested further information from the

Venice police. They reported back that the Venice number belongs to what they call 'a most distinguished family.' ''

Fritz's tone acquired a sardonic lilt. ''The distinguished head of this distinguished family—a Baron Rudolf von Stehlik—told the police that he had indeed been in touch with Dollinger over that period. Because Dollinger was acting as his intermediary in negotiations to purchase a valuable painting owned by a Parisian.''

''What picture? And what is the Parisian's name?''

''The baron declined to contribute that information.''

''And the Venetian police declined to press him for it,'' I guessed.

''Distinguished family,'' Fritz repeated, and smiled.

Jean-Marie Reju was a tall, lean man with wide shoulders, glasses, and a habitual lack of expression. He was wearing the usual unbuttoned raincoat when I ran into him outside the hospital. Reju figured it provided the ideal combination of concealment and swift access for the big Colt .45 he carried on bodyguard jobs. I couldn't tell if he was carrying one now but Reju could always get a permit to, faster than anyone else I knew. Having some pillars of government who wouldn't feel safe traveling abroad without you did help.

He shook my hand without smiling. Life was a serious business to Reju. So was death.

''I thought you were off on a long contract shepherding a Swedish businessman around Europe,'' I said.

''He got sick and went home. I got back this morning and Gregory told me about Fritz. How is he?''

''Coming along pretty well.''

Reju held up a small bouquet of yellow roses. ''I brought this for him.''

It was a surprisingly generous gesture. Reju earned a lot, but was not known for squandering any of it. He valued, and counted, every franc.

''Fritz will be pleased,'' I said, though I wasn't certain he would be. Fritz professed to find Reju irritatingly stupid, an opinion that was based on Reju's lack of humor and that ignored Reju's record of beating him at chess more often than he lost.

"I hope so," Reju said. "It cost thirty francs."

"Inflation. Everybody's complaining about it."

"They should," he said, and with no change of tone: "Have you found the one who shot Fritz?"

"I'm working on it."

"Can I be of help?"

I refrained from saying I couldn't afford his prices. Reju, I'd learned, could get his feelings hurt. "Have you heard anything in the last year or two about an information peddler named Arnaud Galice?"

Reju thought about it. "I'm sorry, I've never come across that name before."

I tried him on what little I knew about the unseen woman who had killed Paul Dupuy in Fritz's place and perhaps Dollinger's girlfriend as well.

Reju gave it careful consideration. He was not one to dispense offhand opinions. "There are a number of female killers around these days," he said slowly. "Political fanatics, most of them. And a few, very few, for hire. But none as good as you say this one is. The ones I know of depend more on their savagery than acquired skill."

He considered some more. Finally he said, "There is a professional bodyguard I worked with a couple times. Isabelle Lachard. A young woman. Most of her jobs involved protecting female clients. She could stick close to them without being conspicuous in circumstances where a man would be. I couldn't accompany a female client into the bathroom, for example."

"It might draw attention," I agreed.

"Yes. This Isabelle Lachard dropped out of the profession a year or so ago. I heard she went abroad somewhere to get married. Or maybe just to live with a man without marriage.

That seems to be increasingly frequent. I don't know what she's doing these days.''

"Something I said made you think of her."

"Isabelle Lachard did carry a knife as a backup weapon. Though I never saw her use it."

"Did she ever kill anybody?"

"Oh, yes. In the performance of her duties. I *hope* she's not your assassin. She seemed a nice young woman."

"But she's good with a gun."

"Very."

"As good as you?" I asked Reju.

"I don't know." It wasn't false modesty. Reju knew he was one of the best in the world, and he assumed everyone else knew it. "We were never on opposite sides. With someone that competent you can't be sure until that happens."

"Would I have a chance against her?"

"No," Reju said soberly. "None at all."

◩ **19** ◪

THE BASEMENT ROOM HAD BEEN TURNED INTO A FULLY
equipped home gymnasium with a bath and dressing room
off to one side. Vents in the walls did a good job of circulating
the air, but a faint aroma lingered: a heady mixture of woman,
sweat, and massage oils. The Kape butler ushered me in and
went away, closing the door behind him.

Susan Kape was on her back on a padded table next to a
rack of free weights. Her crutches leaned against the bench
press unit of a Universal gym machine. Her face, arms, and
legs gleamed with perspiration. Her sleeveless black leotard
was soaked with it.

She was extending her arms over her head, stretching the
springs of a chest pull as far as she could, the muscles of her
arms, shoulders, and neck bunching with the effort. At the
foot of the table her physical therapist, a stocky young woman
in white T-shirt and slacks, was working on her legs. Pushing
against the sole of each bare foot in turn, doubling the leg
back toward Susan Kape's chest.

Even in that awkward position her body was intoxicating.

She relaxed her grip on the chest pull with a loud
"Oooof!" Panting a little, she held it out to me. "Would
you put that somewhere, anywhere for the moment."

I put it on the bench near her crutches.

"My daily workout," she said. "Two long hours of it.

Boring as hell, but it does keep me in shape. I'm not up to jogging anymore, you may have noticed.''

"Try swimming. Not so boring.''

"I do. I've got an indoor pool at my country house outside Paris, and another on Long Island. And when I'm in Florida or Monaco I go in the sea. You have a place near Monaco, don't you?''

"Five minutes away.''

"Good swimmer? You look like you would be.''

"I've been doing it since I could walk,'' I told her. "Bound to be better than when I started.''

"Next time I'm down there maybe we can try swimming together,'' she said. "I always have to have somebody with me, just in case.''

She had her head turned on the padding of the table, watching me as we spoke. The words we were saying to each other didn't mean anything at all. What did was the electricity I'd felt between us the first time: it was still there. Stronger now. My hands got a swollen feeling when I looked at the way her nipples had firmed up, poking into the wet cloth of her leotard.

I reminded myself sternly of the moral and ethical principles involved in any relationship with a client. I also reminded myself that I had no intention of getting sucked into becoming this woman's third husband. Let Yann Bouvier tackle the job of playing against that stacked deck.

"Madame,'' the therapist chided sharply as she pressed against Susan Kape's left foot, "you are not *resisting* me strongly enough.''

"I'm *trying* to,'' Susan Kape growled.

"You must try *harder*. Or the muscles will lose their strength and your legs will no longer be so beautiful.''

I watched Susan Kape wince as her bent left knee was forced back between her breasts. "Hurt a lot?''

"Not more than I can deal with. I take pills against the pain. They make me a little dopey most of the day.'' She looked at me with a crooked smile. "But they give me sexy dreams, too, so I can't complain."

Both of her knees had surgical scars. The scars were short and thin. She would have had the best surgeons, of course; and they would have been paid enough to do their work slowly and carefully, leaving as little external damage as possible.

She saw where I was looking. "That's where the worst of my problem is. I smashed both kneecaps when I fell. Kneecaps, they tell me, are the hardest part of the bone structure to repair or to replace. So far at least they've got me to where I can *stand*. And walk, but not without those lovely crutches for support."

Her grimace had a flash of anger in it. She turned her head and snapped at her therapist, "That's enough for today, Caroline."

"If you say so, Madame." The woman straightened the leg she'd been bending and went into the dressing room.

Susan Kape braced both hands on the padded table and sat up. Then she gripped the backs of her knees and swung her legs off the table. They *were* still beautiful. "Would you fetch me that big towel," she said.

No sentence she started with "Would you" came out sounding like a question. Not a command, either. It was simply that all of Susan Kape's life had taught her to expect affirmative responses.

I got the towel for her. As she used it to wipe her face I said, "Your butler told me Carmen Haung isn't expected in until much later today."

"I sent her off with Yann to do some errands for me." She was silent for a long moment, getting a speculative look. "Of course," she added slowly, "they *could* be using some of the time to do something *else* together . . ." She cocked her head at me. "What do you think, are they playing around with each other?"

"Got no idea."

"But you could find out for me, *if* I wanted you to."

"No," I told her. "I wouldn't be interested."

"Why not? I thought snooping was your business." It ·wasn't meant to be insulting. She was just surprised and curious.

"I don't handle divorces or suspicious lovers," I told her. "Your troubles always turn out to be pretty much the same. No surprises. It's too boring."

"You have a nice, quiet way of showing your temper," she said evenly. "Nothing in the tone, but your eyes get real cold. I like that."

"Like it or don't," I told her. "If you want to find out about your friends, ask them. There are some menial chores you're supposed to handle yourself."

"Yes, *sir*. But I'm not really interested, either. If they're having a thing, let them. I've got no reason to interfere in their fun, when I don't let anyone interfere with *mine*."

There was a short, pregnant silence between us.

Then her physical therapist came out of the dressing room, wearing a long buttoned coat and carrying a satchel. She bade us a courteous farewell and said she'd be back the same time next morning. When she was gone, Susan Kape switched to a businesslike manner.

"Thank you for going down there with Carmen. That little clay figurine she picked at random from the tomb met every test. Authentic—I knew it would be."

"I was pretty sure of it myself," I said. I didn't say anything about *my* figurine. I didn't want anyone being warned off, directly or by inadvertent tone of voice.

"So now there's nothing for me to do but wait," she said, "until they've removed everything from the tomb and gotten it across the border into France."

"They haven't contacted you about when that'll be?"

"No. I tried calling Dollinger's place, but he still isn't there."

That I knew. "Have you ever had contact with any of them, other than Dollinger?"

"Never. I don't have the faintest idea who they are. Or how to get in touch with them, except through him." She began toweling the wet sheen from her arms. "You can send the bill for your time and expenses directly to Piercarlo at our Monaco office. Along with what's owed to Monsieur Donhoff. *And* I'd like that to include all his medical expenses."

"Sounds like you're firing me."

She laughed. "There isn't anything more for you to do that I know of. Now that we're sure I'm not going to be swindled."

"It's not that sure," I said, feeling around the edges of what I had to say. "For example, they could have made copies of everything in the tomb. That would be expensive, but not compared to what they'd get selling you the copies and the real stuff to someone else."

She shook her head. "They won't—and can't. When they deliver it, I'll have more random pieces tested before they get full payment."

"Do they know you're going to do that?"

"Carmen and I told Dollinger. He accepted that condition."

That was interesting. I could think of only two possible reasons for them accepting a condition like that. And I knew one of them was inoperative in this case.

"I'd still like to stay on top of it," I said. "If the money bothers you, you don't have to pay for any further time or work involved. But I want you to let me know the minute Dollinger contacts you again."

Susan Kape regarded me with the start of a teasing smile quirking those luscious lips. "Is it possible you just want an excuse to see more of me?"

My own smile had a certain amount of mockery in it. "That could be a subconscious motive."

"And consciously?"

"It's something I've gotten involved with. I want to stay with it until it's finished."

She'd dropped the smile, studying me with narrowed eyes. "Hell," she said softly, "I wouldn't mind seeing more of you, either . . ." She gripped the edge of the padded table and slid off it until she was standing with her bare feet planted apart on the floor. "Would you help me to the shower. Using the crutches too much chafes my skin."

She slid an arm over my shoulders as I put one of mine across her back to brace her. "You'll have to carry me," she said. "You look strong enough to handle that pretty easily."

I got my other arm under her legs and picked her up. She leaned her softness into my chest as I carried her into the bathroom.

"I think," she murmured softly, "I turn you on."

"You noticed that, did you."

"Ummm . . ." Reaching out a hand, she opened the frosted-glass door of the shower stall. I set her down on her feet inside it.

"Please stand by," she said, closing the door partway, "in case I need help." Twenty seconds later she stuck her leotard out to me. "Like with this. Just hang it on one of the wall hooks."

There were two of those beside the towel rack. I hung the leotard while she closed the door all the way and turned on the shower.

I raised my voice enough to be heard over it. "Do we have an agreement? I stay with the job and you keep me informed?"

"Sure," she called back. "As I said . . ." But she didn't bother finishing it.

After that I listened to the sounds of her showering herself. And avoided looking in her direction for a while. Then I quit denying myself and did look. There wasn't much to be seen through the frosted glass, but my imagination was rampant. That wasn't all that was.

She turned off the shower and opened the door enough to reach out a dripping arm. "A towel, please."

I gave her the biggest one. After a moment she pushed the shower door all the way open. She had wrapped the towel around herself, tying two ends together under her left armpit. She hadn't dried herself much.

She looked up into my eyes, and her own slowly lost that shield that kept you from seeing inside her. "Would you carry me back now?" she asked me in a small voice.

My pleasure. When I picked her up she cuddled against me again, moving her cheek lightly against my ear. I carried her across the gymnasium and set her down on the padded table. She leaned back on one elbow and stared up at me.

I cupped a hand under her chin and bent and kissed that irresistible mouth.

After a time she lay back and her hand reached out to stroke one fingertip softly across my cheek.

Her eyes were shining.

Self-control has its limits. The spirit had already given up the contest and the flesh was more than ready to take over.

I unfastened her towel.

When I left there she was smiling like a contented cat looking forward with lazy confidence to getting her next bowl of cream whenever she got hungry again.

What I was looking forward to was a long shower, a hard drink, and a new set of ethics strong enough to curb an unruly libido. I was confident of the first two, but the third, under the circumstances, felt as remote as peace in our time.

Mainly, I knew, I was mad because I just don't like finding myself doing things I didn't plan on doing. A clear indication of certain deep flaws in my character, as any shrink would be quick to point out. But I didn't need psychoanalysis to tell me that any union of the fallen angels would recognize me as one of their own.

⊠ 20 ⊠

THERE WAS AN ENVELOPE FROM JEAN-MARIE REJU AND A
phone message to call Major Diego Bandini waiting for me
when I returned to my apartment shortly after noon.

I let those wait while I had some of that hard drink. I made
myself a large Scotch on the rocks and took a swallow from
it before having that long shower. By the time I was toweling
myself dry I felt better about my role in recent events.

I reminded myself that I did need to keep Susan Kape
favorably disposed toward me. To make sure she'd let me
know as soon as Dollinger got in touch with her. So I'd be
in a position to manipulate what happened after that.

Also—as Carmen Haung had so rightly pointed out—
Susan Kape *was* pretty overwhelming. Even Sir Gawain had
been known to succumb to temptation when finding himself
entangled with an especially seductive princess.

I put on fresh clothes and found that the ice cubes in my
drink had melted and turned the Scotch watery. Just as well.
I didn't need more hard liquor that early in the day. I emptied
the glass into the sink and put through that call to Diego's
office in Rome.

He told me Aldo had turned up in the police files. "We
would have found his dossier sooner, but we were looking
in the wrong files. Because you were so sure Aldo was a
phony name and he wasn't Italian. He *is* Italian by birth. But

126

when he was ten his parents moved to Belgium with him and a younger sister. He grew up in a Flemish neighborhood of Brussels. That would account for what you thought was a Dutch accent. His full name is Aldo Flavio."

"What put him in your files?"

"He came back in Italy when he was in his forties. He seems to have gotten himself an education in art history by then. He worked here as a guide, taking people on art tours of museums and churches—first in Rome, then in Florence. Then just over five years ago a number of extremely valuable old paintings were stolen from a villa outside Florence. One of the thieves was caught and named Aldo Flavio as the man who'd been fencing the loot for his gang."

"But you didn't catch Aldo," I speculated.

"He skipped the country. What you've told me is the first indication I've come across that he's been back since."

Diego didn't have anything else for me. We promised to keep each other up-to-date, then I made a call to Brussels. To a Belgian private detective named Pauline Jacobs. I'd handled a few inquiries from her in the past, and she'd handled one for me. Both of us had been satisfied with the results.

I told Pauline what I knew about Aldo Flavio, and what I wanted. At the usual fees we charged each other. Double that if she came through in the next two days with something that helped me find Aldo.

Then I opened the envelope from Jean-Marie Reju. Security firms take identification pictures of operatives they hire including those hired on a temporary basis for specific jobs. Reju hadn't had any difficulty getting a copy of Isabelle Lachard's photo from the firm that hired her the two times he had worked with her.

It was a full-face shot. Reju had said she was a nice young woman, and she looked it. Also rather pretty in a quiet way. She'd be thirty now, according to her birthdate on the back of the picture. A wide face with high cheekbones and dark, thick eyebrows that almost met above the bridge of her short, neatly formed nose. Her black hair was cut short around her ears. The expression of her wide eyes and small mouth was direct, honest, with a hint of controlled shyness.

I tried to fit the picture of Isabelle Lachard with the assassin who's spooked me. I couldn't.

Putting her picture in my wallet, I went out to have lunch at a brasserie around the corner in Rue Mouffetard. There was a sign on the wall over the bar: "The New Beaujolais Has Arrived!" The sign was getting old. Like almost everyone in France I'd already sampled the new Beaujolais three weeks ago. But this year's batch was exceptional, and it wouldn't have deteriorated in that short a time. A half bottle of it with a delicious *choucroute garni* added up to a perfect lunch.

I devoted myself to enjoying every bite and sip of it and didn't think about Susan Kape more than five times start to finish.

When I returned to the apartment there was another message from Diego Bandini.

Three hours later I was back in Italy.

21

SAN GIMIGNANO IS A SMALL TUSCAN TOWN WITH A SUR-prising number of stone towers for its size. In the old days each townsman who became reasonably prosperous would add the tallest tower he could afford to his house. For the same reason that he'd buy a new Mercedes today: So his wife could hold up her head when they met the Joneses.

We left the old towers behind us, speeding south from the town following a local police car down past Siena and then west just above Pienza, entering a narrow country road. Diego Bandini was in the backseat of the second car with me, giving me some of the details.

"The local police here received an anonymous phone call telling them where to go. When they got there, they found identification papers on him. Among other items. Since I had circulated the request for information about him, they called me immediately. I phoned you and then raced up here."

He had also managed before leaving Rome to arrange to get me down to this area the fastest way possible. When my plane from Paris had reached the Côte d'Azur airport, a little observation jet supplied by the Italian air force had been waiting to fly me the rest of the way. Diego and his police driver from Rome had picked me up at the military landing strip outside Florence. From there it was a fast drive to San

Gimignano, where the local car stood ready to lead us the rest of the way.

The country road deteriorated as it cut between bleak farms gouged out of low hillsides. Potholes slowed both cars. Diego's driver concentrated on swerving around the worst ones but couldn't avoid all of them. I braced myself against the jolts and asked, "What are those other items found on him?"

"This, for one." Diego handed me what looked like an ordinary file card. On it was written Susan Kape's name, Paris address, and phone number. Below that was Carmen Haung's name. The number beside it was for the phone in her apartment six blocks from the Kape mansion.

"I phoned both of these ladies," Diego said. "Each refused to come down here."

Naturally. As long as they stayed away from Italy for a while, they could even admit what they'd been involved with and not be bothered overmuch by the law because of it. No country gets very upset by the plundering of ancient art treasures that occurs in another country. There are no extradition treaties covering criminal acts of that sort.

The road got worse, turning into a rutted dirt track, leaving the last farm behind and entering an uninhabited area of scrubby woodland. I handed the card back to Diego. "What else?"

He gave me a thick manila envelope. I took out a stack of color photographs.

"Those," Diego said, "were in his pockets."

They were Polaroids, shot with a flash. The first I looked at was of the bronze goddess of Fate statue. The second was of the fresco section that depicted the dead couple smiling at each other. The third was of the gold pectoral. The rest showed other things I'd seen in the tomb. Some were close-ups of individual pieces, others were medium shots of groups of them.

I put the pictures back in the envelope, gave it to Diego, and told him the whole story. Or almost all of it. A few items

I held back, such as the fact that I'd lifted one figurine for testing on my own. I would still need a few secrets to apply leverage in the shadows. But I did fill him in on the rest of it. There was no reason not to now.

I had told the same things to Commissaire Gojon and left out the same small items. He'd driven me out of Paris to Orly Airport personally, to give me the opportunity to do so. By now, I reckoned, he would have gotten the higher authority he needed in order to have a talk with Susan Kape and Carmen Haung. Not enough authority to put any pressure on them of course. Just enough to ask them a few questions politely. I figured they wouldn't mind answering some of them now.

The dirt track became a barely negotiable path and then nothing at all. We followed the lead car into the lower end of a wide ravine and jolted forward until we reached the spot where the way ahead was blocked by a high mound formed from the mudslide. On one side was the wooded slope, on the other the low, bare cliff. I looked back when I climbed out of the car. The pointy hill with the two bare trees on top that I'd spotted two nights ago was there.

Another local police car was parked on our side of the blockage. There was also an ambulance with its rear doors open. The highest-ranking cop there, a lieutenant, hurried over to salute Diego.

"Have they found anything yet?" Diego asked him.

"No, Major. My men are still searching."

Diego nodded at the ambulance. The lieutenant led the way to it. Diego motioned him aside and climbed into the back with me. He told the ambulance attendant inside to open the body bag so we could have a look.

The zipper made a loud, ugly sound as it was dragged all the way open. The attendant pushed the thick plastic aside.

Nobody had closed his eyes. They stared at us out of Friedhelm Dollinger's flabby, deep-lined face. Whenever I'd seen him before, he'd always worn a calm, thoughtful expression, to let you know he was a very serious man. Now he wore an astonished look. Permanently. Or as long as he continued to have a face. Depended on whether they cremated or buried him.

It didn't look to me like the professional work of the spooky assassin. No neatly placed bullet or sure knife thrust this time. The side of Dollinger's skull had been cracked open by some kind of club.

"Any other wounds?" I asked Diego.

"No others. That one was obviously sufficient. Well, is it him?"

"You must have pictures of him in your files."

"I require a positive verbal identification from someone who knew him."

"It's Dollinger," I said.

"Thank you." Diego nodded at the attendant. "You can zip him up and take him away now."

He climbed down out of the ambulance after me and said, "A quarrel between thieves, do you think?" Diego's tone was careless, but his eyes on me were not.

"Or something more calculated," I said. "I think they wanted him found with that card and those photographs on him. I think they wanted the tomb found, too. Which probably means they've gotten everything they could take from it out of the country by now."

"But these men *haven't* found any tomb. Is it here?"

"Get us a couple flashlights," I said.

Diego snapped an order. The lieutenant hurried off to the cars and returned with the flashlights. I led them over the hump and down through the overgrown section of the ravine. Counting off the number of steps I'd memorized two nights before, I turned to the right and had no problem in finding the place where the bushes curtained the doorway into the tomb.

Inside the entrance passage I flashed my light on the

smooth wall. The carving of Charon was still there. It would have taken far too long for the tomb robbers to hack that out of the wall intact.

The first burial vault was empty now except for the stone biers and the few crumbling remnants of wall painting. It was the same in the second chamber. All that remained was the white marble replica of a banquet couch and the segment of fresco in which the dead couple that had been laid on that couch were pictured smiling at each other through eternity.

I rode back to Rome with Diego, who left me in his office working my way through the police files on known *tombaroli*, looking for a picture of "Robby." I didn't find it. By the time I gave up the attempt it was too late to get a flight back to Paris. But Diego returned to his office with an invitation to sleep in his guest bedroom—after sharing a late dinner his wife was preparing at that very moment.

I accepted with pleasure. Diego's wife, in addition to being lovely, smart, and talented, was, I knew from past experience, a mouth-watering cook. The main course she'd conjured up for us that night turned out to be a *minestra di farro*, chock full of calamari, scampi, and *gamberi imperiali* in a sauce of dry white wine. Scrumptious.

Before going to bed we watched the late TV news. The combination of murder, ancient history, and stolen treasure got the tomb story major coverage. It showed blowups of the photographs of the treasure found on Dollinger's body. Also, a television camera team had already taken three Italian experts in Etruscology to investigate the tomb. They were filmed standing before the fresco in the second chamber, giving their expert opinion that they were inside an unquestionable authentic Etruscan tomb. No one, they stated definitely, could have faked that fresco, for example.

Etruscan tombs often acquire names based on what's found in them. There's the Tomb of the Leopards, the Tomb of Hunting and Fishing, the Tomb of the Reliefs. The trio of experts on TV were already referring to this one as the Tomb of the Last Smile.

Over breakfast early next morning we watched a replay of the same TV news coverage, with additional footage flown down from Paris. The new segment was a short interview with Susan Kape and Carmen Haung.

It wasn't difficult to understand why Susan Kape had decided to go along with it. The way she reasoned, the treasure from the tomb had to already be safely on its way to her, probably across the border by now. And the notoriety of a murder being attached to that treasure could only increase excitement about her projected museum acquiring it.

Fairly sound reasoning, except that there was a defect in it that she didn't know about yet.

Carmen Haung was interviewed first, after being introduced as an acknowledged authority on Etruscology, formerly an associate professor at the University of Pennsylvania and an antiquities expert for the art auction firm of Galton-Stallbrass.

Her story was that she'd been approached by Friedhelm Dollinger, whom she knew to be an art dealer of long experience, with a request to check on the authenticity of some Etruscan treasure. The way she'd been taken to the tomb, she said, prevented her from having any idea where it was. She'd examined everything in the tomb and found all of it to be the real stuff. No forgeries. As an added precaution, several of the objects from the tomb, chosen at random, had been put through every kind of scientific testing at the Louvre, where they'd been found to be entirely authentic.

Susan Kape had been interviewed next. She'd parried every tricky question adroitly. Her new museum, named after her late father, *was* expecting to become the recipient of all that newly discovered Etruscan treasure. She had never in her life had anything to do with *smuggling*, not even of a fountain pen. She expected to receive the treasure *in Paris*, and that would be her first contact with it. She intended to pay a fair price for it, get a legal bill of sale for it, and give it the care and display space it deserved. If any other person or government pretended to have prior claim on it, she would want to examine their legal documents proving *they* had purchased it from the original owners, the Etruscans.

She ended the interview with one of her seductive smiles. It seemed to be aimed straight through the TV camera at me.

On my flight to Paris that morning I dozed for a while and had some odd dreams. In them, Susan Kape's smile kept getting mixed up with the smile of an Etruscan noblewoman dead more than two thousand years.

⊠ **22** ⊠

IT WAS A BARE, DUSTY ROOM ON THE THIRD FLOOR OF A
building two blocks from the Place de la Bastille. The curling
edges of long cracks in the linoleum exposed the splintery
dry rot of the wooden flooring underneath. The entire building was empty. The factory that had occupied it for sixty
years had been evicted, and the restoration project that would
turn the building into luxurious apartments had not begun.

Félix Dubuisson sat on a camp bed having a second lunch
out of a cardboard box and a thermos. He was a plump,
entirely bald man with a hawk nose and a cleft chin that stuck
out like the blade of a bulldozer. He was wearing thick red
socks and had his lumber jacket on because there was no
heating in the place. His shoes were on the floor beside a
pair of padded bedroom slippers and two tape recorders with
an attached headset.

"No visitors at all in the last forty hours," he said when
I came in. "Only three phone calls—two in, one out."

"Let me hear them," I said.

Félix swung his short legs off the camp bed, stuffed his
feet into the slippers, and began running one of the recording
reels back. I strolled to the room's single, broken window.
It looked down into a small dirt courtyard with a sawed-off
tree stump in the middle and a couple broken chairs lying

136

beside it. Across the courtyard was the back window of Carmen Haung's second-floor apartment.

"All set," Félix said. I walked back and sat on the camp bed next to him. He handed me the headset and pressed a button. I put one of the earpieces to my ear.

One of the incoming calls was from Yann Bouvier, telling Carmen that an American journalist was coming to the Kape mansion that morning and Susan Kape wanted her there an hour earlier so they could discuss what they were going to tell him. The other was from a stationery shop on Place des Vosges, telling Carmen that the letterheads and cards she'd ordered were ready.

The outgoing call was Carmen telling the shop she would be in to pick up her order at four that afternoon. I checked my watch. Twenty minutes before four.

Félix scanned my face as I handed back the headset. "Nothing, eh? Want me to wrap it up?"

"Not yet. Stick with it another day or two."

"Sure, it's your client's money."

"No," I told him as I headed for the door, "it's my own this time. Remember that when you're making out the bill."

I walked the five blocks. It was a typical Paris winter day. A gray sky hanging low over gray buildings. In the Place des Vosges mommies and nannies were gathering their kids out of the sandbox and taking them home. The stationery shop was under one of the arcades. I sat on a park bench across from it and waited.

About ten minutes later Carmen appeared, striding into the *place* from the direction of the Kape mansion and crossing toward the shop. I intercepted her.

"Where've *you* been?" she asked me. "Susan was trying to reach you, last night and again this morning. Something important she said she had to discuss with you. She asked me if *I* knew where you were."

"I didn't get back until after noon today. I called her an hour ago, didn't she tell you?"

"No, it's been a busy day for me. I haven't seen her since lunch."

What Susan Kape had wanted to discuss was our getting together again. Privately, for strictly personal reasons. On a professional basis she'd had nothing for me at all. "She tells me she still hasn't heard from your tomb robbers. Have *you*?"

"Of course not. I would have told Susan immediately."

"We have to have a talk," I said. "Let's sit down."

"I'm expected at—"

"Now," I said, and took her elbow, steering her over to the bench. Her arm felt rigid.

She tried to loosen up as we sat on the bench. "Do you have any idea *why* Dollinger was murdered?"

I asked a question of my own. "Have you ever been in touch with *any* of the tomb robbers other than Dollinger? Not counting meeting Robby and Aldo the night they took us to the tomb."

"No. Didn't Susan tell you—Dollinger was our only contact."

"It's *your* contacts with them I'm interested in," I said. "The ones you didn't tell Susan Kape about."

"What are you saying?" Carmen asked me in a low voice. She had gone very tense.

I took the little clay figurine out of my pocket and held it in my open hand.

Carmen stared at it in horrified fascination. She would have been a rotten poker player. I watched her face change with each clashing emotion: shock, panic, despair. She had to open her mouth to get air into her lungs. Short, shallow breaths.

"Where did you get that?" she asked raggedly.

"From the tomb. While you were picking up the other one." I dangled mine between thumb and forefinger carelessly. "I had it analyzed. By an expert in Rome."

She looked away at the bare-branched trees around us. Her slim hands closed and pressed against her abdomen. The knuckles of the small fists turned white. "Have you told Susan?" she whispered.

"No."

Her eyes sought my face. "Why not?"

"I'm more interest in striking a bargain with you," I told her. "My silence—in exchange for you telling me the truth."

Her mouth opened and closed. No words came out. She continued staring at me, like a condemned prisoner offered a faint hope of reprieve.

"If I find out you're lying to me," I told her, "or withholding anything—anything at all—I *will* throw you to the wolves. Susan Kape would fire you and tell everyone why. You'd never be able to get another job anywhere in your profession."

"I *know* that," Carmen said desperately.

"So—the truth now?"

I watched her working hard to pull her shattered nerves together, bracing herself before she spoke again. "You don't leave me any choice, do you."

"Some of the background I already know about," I told her. "They thought highly of you at the University of Pennsylvania. You'd have become a full professor eventually. But you got impatient. You didn't want to wait years and years until a professor died of old age and you could move up into his chair. So you went to Galton-Stallbrass in New York, where you believed you'd move up faster."

"You've been talking to somebody in Philadelphia about me."

"And in New York. They thought highly of you at Galton-Stallbrass, too. But only in a subsidiary position. Using your expertise for authenticating pieces and writing glowing descriptions of them for their sales catalogues. That great career you told me you gave up to come work for Susan Kape—it didn't exist. You'd have gone on working behind the scenes under other people—many as young as you or younger."

"Debutantes," Carmen said bitterly, "with hardly any professional credentials at all. They had more pull at Galton-Stallbrass than I could ever hope for."

"Sure. The hardest thing for any auction house to get hold of is something to auction in quantity. And they're all competing with each other to get it. Antique furniture, jewelry, art—heirlooms owned by old rich families. The most valuable employees an auction house can have are ones with a lot of personal connections with those families—people from the same kind of families."

Carmen was silent, her mouth tight with remembered disillusion and anger.

"So you jumped at the chance to come over and put Susan Kape's museum together for her. You thought she was going to make you its director. But you discovered finally that *she* intends to run it. With you helping behind the scenes again. Working, again, for someone with no professional credentials. Just a lot of money and the right kind of family background.

"That made you ripe when somebody came along with a scheme for swindling some of that money out of her. How much of it did they promise you?"

Carmen didn't answer at first. I dangled the fake figurine again, swinging it slightly by its head. She watched as though hypnotized by it. Then she said dully, "A hundred thousand dollars . . . It seemed . . . I . . ." She stopped and drew a deep breath, getting her voice back under control. "I think it was for a kind of revenge, as much as the money. But I didn't *dream* anything like what's happened would come of it. Monsieur Donhoff being shot . . . That girl killed in Dollinger's place . . ."

"But it didn't scare you enough to make you back out of the deal."

"How could I? It was too late by then. I was terrified they'd get even with me by revealing my part in it."

"The tomb *is* authentic," I said, watching her inquiringly. "But it was looted long ago."

"Perhaps as long ago as the Roman conquest," Carmen said quietly. "Certainly before the first landslide covered the way in."

"Everything we saw in the tomb—everything the gang took out of it—is as phony as *this*." I bounced the little clay figurine in my palm.

Carmen just nodded.

I put the figurine back in my pocket. "The three pieces that met the tests were the *only* genuine Etruscan ones. The two Dollinger lent you and Susan Kape, and the one Robby signaled you to choose when we were in the tomb. Somebody with Dollinger's connections wouldn't have any trouble getting hold of a few authentic pieces. What they had to pay for that—and for making all the fake stuff—was nothing compared to the eventual payoff.

"And," I added, "they *wanted* someone like me to come to the tomb with you. As a witness that you picked that last piece *at random*. Am I right so far?"

Again Carmen just nodded.

"Okay," I said, "we're back to my main question. Were you ever in contact with any of the gang other than Dollinger?"

I was paying close attention to Carmen's expression and voice.

She said, "No."

I went on looking at her.

She shook her head emphatically and repeated the one word: "No."

I said, "Shit."

She misread my anger. "It's the *truth*."

"I believe you," I said. "That's the trouble. Everything you know about the swindle you got from Dollinger. But he didn't know everything. Because he certainly didn't expect to wind up dead. Somebody else in the gang planned that."

"Why?"

"So the tomb would be found. And found to be authentic, by experts. So the photographs of everything they'd taken out of it would be found on his body, and shown to the world. So *you* would say you'd examined all of it and found it all to be genuine."

I was silent for a while, chewing on the part of it I liked least. I said it out loud finally. "And Dollinger's death also means neither you nor Susan Kape are likely to *ever* hear from the rest of the gang."

"What do you mean?" Carmen asked, puzzled. "They have to get in touch with us in order to sell what they have to us."

"I think," I said, "that your boss wasn't the fish they planned to catch. I think she was just the bait."

"I don't understand," Carmen said.

But I didn't explain the rest of it to her.

◪ 23 ◪

Fritz was on the phone when I got to his hospital room.

"That may prove to be useful," he was saying to whoever was at the other end of the line. "Thank you. If you learn anything further, please call me again." He listened to a question and answered it. "They want to keep me here another week. I expect to cut that in half. If I'm not here I'll be back at my apartment . . . Yes, thank you again."

He put the phone down on the table next to him and leaned back with a soft grunt against the cranked-up head of his bed. "One of my Vienna contacts," he told me. He sounded cheerful, but his voice hadn't regained its customary vigor yet. "With information about Baron Rudolf von Stehlik. You do remember the baron, I assume."

"I remember the police regard him as the distinguished head of a distinguished family—in Venice."

"But as I suspected from his name, he is originally from Austria."

"Fritz," I said, "according to your doctor you're not supposed to strain yourself doing anything remotely connected with work. Even using the phone, except to assure friends you're okay."

"In my lengthy experience, my boy, doctors seldom know best. I'll die of sheer boredom just lying here listening to my

143

heartbeat. So I attempted to give you a little assistance. You seem to need it.''

I sat down by his bed and gave up trying to reinforce doctor's orders. The fact was, I did miss having Fritz's vast network to depend on. It was taking me too long to dig up information he could get with a single call on the phone.

I gestured at the one beside his bed. ''What did you get for me?''

''The Baron von Stehlik is in his early sixties, with a history in Vienna of being something of a ladies' man. His family there *is* a distinguished one, not too wealthy but not poor either, and with a long history. But the distinguished family the police in Venice meant is the Italian one he married into ten years ago. The Valmarano family. Von Stehlik is now considered the head of it because it has no other male member left. There was only his wife, who died two years ago, and her older maiden sister, who lives in the Valmarano palazzo with the baron.''

''Anything else?''

''I expect to have his exact address for you before you leave for Venice.''

''You think I should go there,'' I said.

''Definitely.'' Fritz had the faintly smug look he sometimes got when he was holding back the zinger.

I figured he was entitled to some fun, so I went along with it and played straight man for him. ''Because von Stehlik was in phone contact with Dollinger about a painting he won't identify?''

''That's one reason.''

''And the other?''

''I made a call to Pauline Jacobs in Brussels,'' Fritz told me, drawing out the suspense more.

''I tried to reach her a couple hours ago,'' I said. ''She wasn't at home or at her office.''

''My call was less than twenty minutes ago. She'd just gotten back from Ostend. That is where Aldo Flavio's younger sister lives now with her husband and three children. She told Pauline her brother never discusses what he's doing, nor where, on the rare occasions when she sees him. She hasn't seen him at all since he visited Belgium last Christmas. But he always sends a card for her birthdays.''

I just waited until Fritz got tired of holding it back.

"Her last birthday was three weeks ago," he told me. "The card she got from Aldo was sent from Venice."

That's the way the peculiar business I'm in functions eighty percent of the time. You tug at every loose thread you can find in a tangled tapestry. Eventually one of them may come out attached to something of interest. If it interrelates with something that's turned up before, you've got a lead worth following.

24

THEY'VE BEEN CALLING VENICE A MARRIAGE OF CITY AND sea for some ten centuries. Which one's the bride depends on how you see it. The way I'd been seeing it for the past two days, Venice was—reluctantly. And what the sea was doing to it resembled a rape more than a wedding.

Venetians refer to what was going on as *aqua alta*—a rise in sea level flooding their town until it's hard to distinguish the hundred and fifty canals from the pedestrian streets and squares around them. Only the hundreds of short, high-humped bridges that cross the canals remain above a bad inundation.

Below my window in the Pensione Cesare local citizens splashed through calf-deep water, making their way across a little *campo* between equally flooded shops and passages. None of them looked overly concerned. Venice gets that way five to ten times each year. Regular residents expect it, accept it as an act of God on a par with overlong TV commercials, and deal with it by simply keeping a pair of knee-high rubber boots ready at home for use when it happens.

I got into my own rubber boots before leaving my room. I'd bought them from one of the vendors outside the cavernous multilevel garage at the end of the causeway from the mainland. That was where I'd parked my car, because the only way to ride beyond that point in central Venice is via boat.

The trip from Paris would have been much quicker if I'd flown all the way to the airport outside Venice. But that way I couldn't have brought along a few items that I thought might be essential to my having a future. So I'd flown down to the Côte d'Azur, taxied home, hidden those few items in my Peugeot, and driven five and a half hours to Venice. I'd figured the gambling odds were with me. I had never had a car searched crossing the frontier from France into Italy, and my luck stood up again.

One of the items I'd smuggled across the border was holstered on my belt when I left my room. It was concealed by my jacket and also by the loose-hanging raincoat I'd bought along with the boots. I didn't need the raincoat that afternoon. It wasn't raining out. The sun was shining on the water-logged city out of an absolutely clear sky. But I'd bought it to conceal one of the other items. Though I wasn't carrying that one today I wanted people to get accustomed to seeing me wearing the raincoat. For when it became necessary.

Actually, I was fairly certain nobody was paying that kind of attention to me as yet. That, however, was about to change. Two days had been wasted keeping tabs on Baron von Stehlik's place, without spotting anyone I was looking for. Instruction number three in the private-eye manual says: When you can't find the people you're after, do something to make them come after you.

Below my room I had three flights of stairs to negotiate. Each step sagging, creaking, tilting, and covered—partially—by worn-out carpeting. The Pensione Cesare had spacious rooms with comfortable beds and was spotlessly clean. But, like almost all of Venice, it was in an advanced state of collapse.

A huge police dog named after the Pensione was resting his bulk on the third step from the bottom. He raised his heavy head when I maneuvered very carefully around him. I didn't pat it, though I'd known him on and off since he was a large puppy. Cesare wasn't raised to be a pet.

The little lobby was only ankle-deep in floodwater. I waded across it and hung my key on the rack beside the desk. I could see the two elderly ladies who ran the place closed in the glass-doored room behind the desk, watching TV with their booted legs up on a table. They didn't notice me and didn't have to. If I'd been somebody that Cesare hadn't watched sign the Pensione register, he would have bounded over with a noise louder than a bark and scarier than a growl.

That was one reason I liked to use the pensione when I was in town on business. Difficult for a stranger to come in at me past Cesare. Another reason was that the Pensione Cesare wandered through two old buildings joined together. That gave me three ways in or out. One to the *campo*, another into an alleyway, the third to the *calle* alongside a narrow canal. And none of the three was in sight of the other two.

This time I went through a back passage, crossed a tiny, forlorn garden enclosed by the backs of the two buildings, and took another passage out to the narrow canal. The high banks of houses on both sides of it kept out the sun, and a cold draft blew through it. I waded quickly along the *calle* through water at the same level as the surface of the canal beside it.

I didn't slow down until I emerged onto the wide Riva Degli Schiavoni facing the San Marco Basin. The Riva was covered with water, too, but it was also drenched in the warming sunlight that Venice expects on more days than not until after Christmas. I strolled to the nearest *vaporetto* landing station and waited there in the sun.

The water bus came along ten minutes later, disgorging half of its passengers. I was among the first of the new cluster of passengers boarding it. I didn't give too much attention to the others.

The *vaporetto* swung past the Ducal Palace and the Molo approach to the city's biggest square, the Piazza San Marco.

We passed a couple barges, and a speeding motor launch passed us, and then we were chugging by the dome of the Salute into the Grand Canal. Two stops later I got off. I left the landing by way of a covered alleyway, and I didn't look back to check on anyone coming off after me.

Baron von Stehlik lived in the Santa Croce district, in a palazzo that had known better days. His entrance doorway was on one side of an elongated square that had an iron-capped well of eroded stone in its center. The sculptured marble columns framing his doorway were ravaged by the same source of erosion: sulfuric gases wafted from the mainland factories on the other side of the lagoon around Mestre.

Across the *campo* from the baron's place was an even older palazzo. Its ground-floor space was now occupied by a trattoria, a pharmacy, and several food stores. Above them flood-drenched carpets had been hung out to drip-dry, on clotheslines stretched between windows that retained traces of their former Romanesque beauty. I got hit on the head by two fat drops from one of the carpets as I went into the trattoria.

All of the tables inside were taken by regular customers having their afternoon coffees and political arguments as though unaware that their booted feet were submerged in brownish water. I took a place at the end of the short bar and ordered an espresso.

There was a framed picture on the wall near me, showing gondolas gliding across the Piazza San Marco. It kicked the pins out from under the theory of some scientists that the Venetian floods were caused by recent increases in the tides of the Adriatic Sea. The picture was a Tironi painting done back in 1825, so the *aqua alta* wasn't exactly a new phenomenon.

The radio behind the bar was broadcasting the news. By careful listening I was able to make out why the announcer sounded so cheerful. The good news was that the high tide was now receding. By next morning, the announcer rhapsodized, Venice should once more be the "floating city" so beloved by romantic poets down through the ages.

Nobody in the trattoria acted as if he cared one way or the other about whether the city was drowning or floating. Most of the impassioned arguments continued to focus on the latest atrocity of the Red Brigades terrorists: the bombing of a train filled with families traveling to their hometowns to make early preparations for the Christmas holiday.

I took a sip of my hot, strong espresso and looked through the trattoria's window to the palazzo where Baron von Stehlik lived. Several of its Byzantine-Gothic windows were bricked up. More than half of the slabs of colored marble that had covered the wall when it was truly palatial had flaked off, leaving exposed areas like reddish-brown scabs.

This had been the rear of the palazzo in the time when the Italian family the baron had married into owned all of it. Back then the entrance had been around the other side facing a canal inside the Valmarano landing dock, with its mooring posts where visitors of equal rank and fortune could tie up their privately owned gondolas.

But the Valmarano family had diminished in wealth as it decreased in number, making it necessary to sell off sections of the palazzo. Much of it was now subdivided into office complexes, apartments, and two smart shops. In these reduced circumstances the baron and his sister-in-law were confined to the rear of the dismembered palazzo in living quarters not much bigger than a normal house for a family of ten. The baron, as Fritz had learned, was not rich, but not exactly poor, either.

I finished my coffee and scanned the trattoria. The stocky, freckled man I was looking for hadn't come in. Nor, when I surveyed the corners and doorways of the *campo* outside, could I spot a much taller, dour-faced man.

Both of them remaining invisible meant two things. One: Nobody I had to worry about had followed me from the Pensione Cesare. Two: None of the people I wanted to find had gone into or come out of the baron's place in the last three hours.

So the time had come to do what had to be done.

I left the trattoria, waded across the square, and did some hammering on Baron von Stehlik's heavy brass doorknocker.

⊠ **25** ⊠

THE ROOM WAS PLEASANTLY WARM AFTER MY WAIT IN AN
entrance hallway as cold as a grave and a climb up two flights
of wide, drafty stairway. The warmth issued from a kerosene
heater that had been installed inside a massive fireplace of
green marble. Baron von Stehlik used the room as his studio.
The only furniture was a mahagony desk, two old armchairs,
and a tall open cabinet beside the easel at which the baron
had been working. Yellowing lace curtains were drawn across
the large window to partially veil the view of office windows
across a small interior courtyard. The room's ceiling was a
slanting skylight of grimy glass panels. A pigeon had settled
on one of the panels and died of old age shortly before I'd
arrived.

"Do you like it?" von Stehlik asked me as he cleaned the
brush he'd been using.

He didn't mean the dead pigeon. He was referring to the
canvas on his easel. So far what he'd done to it was a slash
of cobalt across a dark red square on a chalky-white background.

"Interesting," I said. It wasn't bad, if you like minimalist
abstracts. I don't, much. There were finished canvasses of
the same kind leaning against two walls. Hung on a third
wall were several from the baron's preminimalist period.
Nudes of young girls in what were intended to be provocative

152

poses. The intention failed abysmally because the baron was rotten at conveying any sense of human flesh and articulation. The girls looked like obscene, badly constructed dolls.

"I'm just a dabbler, of course," he informed me. "No formal training at all. My father discouraged my interest in the arts. He wanted me to be a sensible banker."

He'd chosen to converse in English, after learning that it and French were the only languages in which I was fluent. Baron von Stehlik was fluent in English, French, German, Italian, Hungarian, Spanish, and Portuguese. Another of his accomplishments was having entered his sixties with his handsome profile and strong body fairly intact. The honey-colored hair hadn't thinned much and had only a suggestion of silver in it. There seemed to be very little fat under the paint-stained jogging suit he was wearing.

I said, "But obviously your interest in the arts remained in spite of that, *Commendatore*."

He smiled at my use of his new honorary title. "Ah, you know about that."

I nodded. The Italian government had bestowed the honor on him in gratitude for his encouraging Venetian craftsmen by staging a festival of their best work once a year in the ground-floor rooms of the palazzo. "You must know every artisan in town by now," I said respectfully. "The jewelers, goldsmiths, wood carvers, glassmakers, and so on."

"Not only those here in Venice," he told me, putting his brush down neatly on the cabinet next to his palette. "I would say I'm acquainted with all the really good ones in the rest of the Veneto, as well. Vicenza, Treviso, Verona, Asolo, Padua. They all come to display their wares at my annual festival."

He moved over to the desk and pointed to a sculptured silver box on it. "Some of them are touchingly grateful. This, for example. The work of a superb artisan from Asolo. A present to thank me for introducing him to potential clients."

Von Stehlik opened the box. It was wood-lined and filled

with thin cigars. He selected one, lit it, and shut the box without offering me one. Dropping the match into a bronze ashtray adorned with two mermaids, he settled into one of the armchairs. He didn't suggest I sit down in the other.

"Now then," he said, "about poor Friedhelm Dollinger. I know of his unpleasant death, naturally, from the news. I did know him as an art dealer of some experience. I bought a couple paintings through him in the past, and I was recently considering purchasing another. Not the works of the great masters. I can no longer afford that. But quite good, of their kind. And I found Dollinger's prices reasonable. I was, of course, startled to learn he may have been in some way associated with that group of tomb robbers."

"Did you ever introduce Dollinger to any of the local artisans you know?" I asked him.

His heavy-lidded eyes narrowed. "I don't understand— what are you trying to find out?"

"Suppose what the gang took out of the tomb was a bunch of recent forgeries. They'd need some good craftsmen to make convincing forgeries of all of it."

Von Stehlik tapped cigar ash into the bronze tray. "According to the news media and the experts interviewed, everything in that tomb was genuine."

"I don't think so," I told him.

He sucked at his cigar and blew out a plume of smoke. "If you've come here for my opinion about some unsupported conjecture you're pursuing, I'm afraid I can't be of any help. I've never been good at guessing games. Nor interested in them." He glanced at his watch pointedly. "As I told you when you arrived, you *are* interrupting me. If you've anything further to ask me, please do so and let me get back to my painting."

He hadn't answered the first question, and I didn't expect answers to any others. That wasn't what I'd come there for. I took out two snapshot-sized photographs. One was a copy of the full-face picture Diego's agent had taken of Aldo. The other was a copy of the one Reju had gotten for me of Isabelle Lachard.

I put them on the desk next to von Stehlik. "Do you know either of these people?"

There was another narrowing of the eyes as he studied the pictures briefly. "No."

"The woman's name is Isabelle Lachard," I told him. "The man is Aldo Flavio."

"Never heard of them."

"Perhaps if I could show these to your sister-in-law—"

"Even if I were to allow you to question her," von Stehlik interrupted, "she could be of no help. She has been a sick woman for several years, and one of her illnesses is a failure of her eyesight."

"There's another man I'm looking for," I said. "A Frenchman named Arnaud Galice."

"That name doesn't mean anything to me, either," the baron said impatiently, and got rid of more cigar ash.

"He's probably using another name now," I said, and gave him the description I'd gotten from Fritz: lean, thin-faced, with black hair and pointy beard, and the barely perceptible fault in the way he walked.

"I must have seen dozens of men over the years who would answer that vague a description," von Stehlik said.

"Then I've wasted my time coming here. And yours. Sorry about that." I shrugged and gestured at the pictures on his desk. "Maybe I'll have better luck with the posters."

"Posters?"

"I gave copies of these to a printer to be made into posters—together with my reward offer for anyone who does know anything about either of these people. The posters will be ready in two days. I'll spread them around town and see what happens."

Von Stehlik crushed his cigar out in the ashtray. "Why are you telling me this?"

I gave another shrug. "Just thought it was interesting."

"Not to me. So now if you will—"

He was interrupted by the return of his servant, a thickset young man with the fair coloring of many people in northeast Italy. He was the one who'd brought me up here. This time he had on canvas workgloves and was carrying a folded stepladder.

"That took you *long* enough," von Stehlik snapped at him in Italian. "When I tell you to do something, Carlo, I expect you to do it *promptly.*"

"Sure, Baron," Carlo said in a bored tone. He set up the ladder under the skylight and began climbing it.

"Not only is he lazy," von Stehlik told me in French, "but he is also *surly.*"

When he saw me glance up at Carlo, he said, "Don't worry, he doesn't understand French." He grimaced and added, "The servants you can get these days—I had a wonderful old man for years, but he died six months ago. Forcing me to take what I could get. Believe me, this one I'll fire as soon as I can find someone better."

I stuck to English, because I'd learned coming in that Carlo did understand that. "My name and phone number are on the back of these photographs."

"So?"

We were both watching Carlo, who was opening a panel in the skylight near the dead pigeon.

"I'm prepared," I said, "to pay good money for information about these two people."

"I *told* you," von Stehlik reminded me irritably, "I don't know either of them."

Carlo reached out with a gloved hand and picked up the dead pigeon. As he started to come down with it, von Stehlik snapped at him, "You left some of its feathers up there!"

Carlo muttered something nasty under his breath and boosted himself up again. He put the dead pigeon down on top of the ladder and reached out onto the skylight for the offending feathers.

Baron von Stehlik got to his feet and told me bluntly, "It's time for you to go. *Now.*"

To make sure of it, he escorted me himself: down the drafty stairway, through the dark, cold entry hall, and out the door. The door shut behind me with a thump that bounced its brass knocker.

But he hadn't told me to take my photographs away with me. Those were still up there on his desk.

What that meant to me was that I'd probably achieved what I'd gone in there for.

With maybe an added bonus.

⊠ 26 ⊠

THE BONUS CAME THROUGH FIRST. A PHONE CALL TO MY pensione that night from Carlo.

We met in a café in the Calle del Paradiso. Behind the covered fish and produce markets at the west of the high, columned Rialto Bridge that connects the two main islands of central Venice. With the markets closed for the night the jumble of dark alleys and canals in the Rialto district was almost deserted. A tourist couple from Norway were the only other customers in the café. Our table was in its opposite corner, where we could talk freely over the brandies I bought for us.

"How *much*," Carlo asked after our drinks arrived, "is what you called *good money* today in the baron's studio?"

"*Do* you know the people whose pictures I left on his desk?"

"The man, not," he said. "You see, I am honest. But the girl, yes. I see her three, four times. Visiting the baron. With a man—not the man of the photo—another." He took a long sip from his glass while he eyed me shrewdly. Then he repeated, "How much is *good money*?"

I counted five twenty-dollar bills onto our table between our drinks. "One hundred American dollars," I said. Being American dollars would give the amount more value in Carlo's eyes. He could trade that on the local black market for much more than the official bank rate of exchange.

"That," I explained, "is just for recognizing her. You get another two hundred American dollars if you have anything to say about her that I find of interest. Fair?"

I put my glass down on the five bills and held it there while I watched his face: greed to take what was offered struggling with a natural inclination to try bargaining the price up. "*That's* the offer," I told him. "It won't go up a penny. But if I like what you tell me, I won't pretend I don't. You'll get the rest."

Carlo finally nodded. "Fair."

I took my glass off the first hundred. Carlo folded it neatly and stuck it in his breast pocket with a happy smile.

I shifted my chair a little. Enough so I could talk with Carlo and watch the café's door at the same time. Isabelle Lachard visiting the baron that often made it almost certain. She *was* the spooky assassin, and she was around here. From now on I had to walk scared. I wanted her, but I didn't want to die of her.

"The man she came to visit the baron with," I said, "what's he look like?"

"Skinny man. Little beard." Carlo used his two forefingers to draw a beard just below his own blunt chin, bringing the fingertips together. Short, pointy beard.

I gave him the rest of the description of Arnaud Galice, as Fritz had told it to me. He concentrated on it, then shook his head. "It *sounds* like him. Could be. But maybe not. You see, I *am* honest, I don't pretend. If he is limping, I didn't see it."

"What did the baron call him? His name."

"I never heard that. Not the name of the girl, also. But it *is* her in the photo. I look at her, more than the man." Carlo grinned, one man to another. "Nice. Gentle. Soft and sweet, I think. I like her. The baron, he like her also. In that way. I see him look at her. But she— she is nice to him, but not the way he would like. She— I hear she is sister to the man she comes with. But that, I think, is a lie. To make the stupid baron hope. *I* think the man she comes with is her man— husband or man friend, you know. This I only *think*, I am not sure.''

''How long ago did they first come to see the baron?''

''I see them there, oh, three months, maybe four months ago. But I think they were there before. Only I didn't see.''

''When did you see them there the last time?'' I said.

''A week ago. Or maybe nine days.''

It was so dark outside the café door that it would be impossible to get a quick, clear look at anybody who was between me and the door, but that wouldn't save me. Not if it was Isabelle Lachard out there. *She* could probably put a bullet between Carlo's earlobe and shoulder and into my heart without pausing to take dead aim.

I dropped my right hand down to my thigh, closer to my pistol. It was the compact Heckler & Koch P7 I usually kept hidden in my Peugeot. Extensive use had proved it to be extremely accurate. But that wouldn't be enough. Not in a pistol-shooting match with her. I wished I had that other item I'd brought to Venice with me then in the café.

I did have another form of insurance, outside. But against Isabelle Lachard that might not be enough either.

''What else did you hear them talk about?'' I said. ''Beside's hearing she was supposed to be the man's sister.''

Carlo studied me, his mind working quickly behind the eyes. I looked back at him and felt my facial muscles tighten, turning my look into a cold stare. His mind slowed down. He sighed.

''Nothing,'' he admitted, miserable about it as he envisioned the other two hundred sailing away without him. ''They go in the baron's library to talk private. Shut door.''

''You never listened through the door?''

''I try. No good. Thick door. I hear voices, but not what

they say. I know the man with the girl, *he* talks most." Carlo suddenly remembered something. "Ah. But two times, they come with *another* man. Old. Fat. Soft face. He talks also. In the library." Another sigh. "But I don't hear what."

I got a small photo from my pocket. With my left hand. This one Commissaire Gojon had given me.

Carlo looked at it and nodded immediately. "Yes. *Him.*"

It was a picture of Friedhelm Dollinger.

I put it away and questioned Carlo a while longer. But he had given me all he had. He sweated it until I put the other two hundred on the table. Then he broke out another happy smile, tucked the money in with the first hundred, gulped the rest of his drink thirstily, and left.

I gave Carlo five minutes to get some distance away. Then I paid for our brandies and stepped out into the Venetian night. Nobody at all was in sight out there. I turned in the direction of my pensione and began walking.

There was nothing I could do now but wait to see if my threat to spread posters of Isabelle Lachard and Aldo around town drew blood.

It wasn't a long wait.

About twenty minutes.

⊠ 27 ⊠

I CLIMBED ACROSS THE RIALTO BRIDGE VIA ITS CENTRAL PASsage, between the rows of closed shops in its high columned arcades. Up the steps to the middle, down more steps to the other side of the Grand Canal. When they built the Rialto four hundred years ago, they wanted it high enough for the biggest Venetian battle galleys to sail under with their masts up. From the bridge I turned toward the Merceria.

That was the main pedestrian thoroughfare between the Rialto and San Marco, and the quickest way for me to get through that part of the city in the direction of my pensione. But I didn't stick with the Merceria. It was too well lit to suit me. I left it at the next opening.

After that I worked my way through a series of obscure side routes using short passages, crooked canals, and little bridges. My detour switched directions constantly, sometimes after only ten steps. The intricate labyrinth of Venice is easy to get lost in at night. But I'd already used this same zigzag route that night, coming in the other direction for my rendezvous with Carlo.

Its darkness gave me a measure of protection, making me an indistinct target. It also allowed me to walk with my gun held ready in my fist. During tourist seasons I would have kept meeting other people, most of them ones who'd gotten disoriented trying to find their way back to their hotels. But at this time of winter there was absolutely nobody in sight that late.

The news broadcasts had been right. The flood level was going down. The water I walked through now didn't come more than halfway up to the ankles of my boots. But it was impossible not to make a splashing noise with each step, audible for some distance in that total night silence. Several times I halted abruptly. Once I heard two splashes in the murk behind me, before the walker following the same route back there could come to a stop.

I moved on with the comforting solidity of the H & K pistol hanging down by my thigh, letting it swing a little like a pendulum weight. When I neared the Piazza San Marco, I switched direction again to detour around it. All along the way I avoided even the smallest *campos*. They were all bathed in the moonlight that suffused the domes and spires above with a pearly glimmer.

Twenty minutes after leaving the Rialto behind I was approaching the pensione.

Each of its three entrance doors would be locked this late, but I had taken my guest keys along with me. This time I intended to enter through its alley door. Because that was how I'd arranged to return, before I'd left the pensione to meet Carlo.

I went through a covered passage that cut under a conglomeration of houses in that direction. At the other end was a short arch of brick bridge without railings. It led directly into the pensione's alley, on the other side of a minor canal with no walkway on either bank. The attached houses rose straight up out of the water on both sides.

I stepped out of the covered passage onto the bridge and was taking my second step over it when a pinpoint of light blinked on and off inside the alley on the other side. It was too tiny and too quick to be noticed unless you were watching for it. I was.

It jolted me into the fastest evasive action available to me in that exposed position.

I went off the bridge into the canal. Not a dive; there was no time for that. I just threw myself off and struck the water with a great resounding splash.

I didn't hear the shot that came a split second later. But I felt it fan past my head and saw the slug kick up a little geyser when it hit the surface of the canal in front of me.

I sucked my lungs full of air and went under, dragging myself down until I was touching the soupy mud at the bottom. Stuffing the pistol in my belt, I turned to my right and swam along the bottom until I got stopped by an underwater wall. It was a close-set row of posts—Dalmation oak. Most of the buildings of Venice rest on that kind of piles, driven deep into the clay beneath the lagoon's bottom mud.

Staying submerged, feeling my way along the piles, I followed the canal to the left, going with the sluggish current moving through it. Judging by the way the first bullet had plunged into the water, it had come from high above. From a roof or an upper window overlooking the little bridge. That told me where that sniper was, roughly. But not whether there were others, nor where they might be.

I did know one thing: I had to get as far from there as I could before I surfaced to take my next breath.

At times like that I could be grateful to Babette for getting me into long-distance swimming so young. Sticking with it ever since had developed lungs that could survive underwater longer than most. I concentrated on remembering the exact layout of the immediate neighborhood while I felt my way past the thick submerged piles.

When I came to the end of that row of them, I knew where I was. At that point a sliver of a canal connected up with the one I'd jumped into. It was little more than an alley of water, but when I turned into it I found it to be as deep as the other.

I swam the length of it, touching one side or the other with every stroke. It seemed a long haul, though I knew it wasn't. My lungs were beginning to notify me that they did need air from time to time. Nobody's lungs can hold out forever and no amount of practice can reequip them to breathe water.

At the far end of my sliver of canal—as I remembered it—there'd be a low bridge. When I calculated that I'd swum that far, I cautiously raised myself until my face was just above the water. And let my tortured lungs have some of the air they were demanding, without letting them be too noisy about it.

I *was* underneath the bridge. Shrouded in its shadow, I took some more slow, quiet breaths while I pulled the gun from my belt. I brought it up above the surface, tilting its barrel down to shake the water out. I knew it should still work. Should. It hadn't been immersed too long. But you can never be smugly certain about something like that. Not when your life depends on it. Which is why atheist combat soldiers find themselves suddenly given to prayer on occasion.

Beyond the bridge that concealed me was a somewhat wider canal. My lungs didn't need any further time off. Or so I told them. I rolled over on my back and used just my legs to scissor my way silently out from under the bridge. Keeping my pistol above water with my finger across the trigger and the barrel tilted up now. As I emerged from the shadow of the bridge I swiftly scanned both sides of the canal.

On one side the houses had no separation between their foundations and the water. Their windows were all shuttered, and I couldn't spot anyone atop any of the roofs. On the other side was a narrow quay that seemed deserted. But the quay was also too dark to be sure.

A situation calling for another small prayer. To whatever gods may be. And no life lives forever . . .

I angled over to the quay. Hooked my left arm over the edge and then swung the rest of me up onto it as fast as I could. I was getting my feet under me when I thought I saw movement in the black entrance of a passageway.

The movement became definite, and more violent, while I was still trying to bring my pistol around in that direction. A man erupted from the passage with a compact submachine gun. An Uzi or MAC-10, from the brief look I got before it dropped out of his hands and clattered on the cobbles of the quay. He stumbled past it into a patch of moonlight with his legs bending and his arms dropping and his face gone utterly slack.

Nobody I knew. I saw that much in the moment before he fell into the canal.

⊠ **28** ⊠

JEAN-MARIE REJU STEPPED OUT OF THE DARK PASSAGE, lowering the big Colt .45 he'd clubbed the man with.

He kicked the man's weapon into the water. It sank. The man didn't. He was floating, with his face down in the water and his arms and legs stretched out loosely, drifting away in the sluggish tide of the canal.

"That leaves three," Reju told me softly in that unemotional voice of his. "They spread out to look for you."

"Including the first shooter?" I whispered back.

"The man on the roof. Yes, he came down." Reju nodded toward the floater. "This one was in a corner of the *campo*, watching the front door there. That's clear for you now."

Reju faded back into the passageway and its darkness swallowed him up.

In spite of his assurance, I didn't get careless at any point along the way in my slow and roundabout approach to the pensione's *campo* entrance.

Cesare prowled out of the shadowy corridor behind the lobby as I came in and regarded me thoughtfully. I headed for the stairway on legs that were still quivering. The dog turned around and slunk back into the gloom from which he'd come.

I climbed the steps without switching on the stairway

167

lights. Once inside my room lights were okay. I'd left the shutters and curtain closed when I'd gone out.

The first thing I did after locking myself in was to field-strip my Heckler & Koch, spread all the pieces out on the table, and use a bathroom towel to dry each one thoroughly. Without taking off my soggy clothing beforehand. Training will tell.

Then I unlocked the bottom drawer of the dresser, pulled it all the way out, and took a canvas bag out of the dresser space under the drawer. I unzipped the bag, took a small oilcan and a soft cloth from it, and worked over the pieces of the gun with that, including the magazine and bullets.

By the time I reassembled the pistol, my clothes and I had spread a number of wide puddles on the carpet. I finally stripped myself, tied the towel around my middle, and started running a hot bath. Padding barefoot out of the bathroom, I got the next item out of the canvas bag.

It was a pump-action shotgun with a short barrel and a pistol grip. And a sling for hanging it from my shoulder down my side under the raincoat.

The other stuff in the bag was ammunition for the pistol and the shotgun. The pistol was already loaded. I inserted one of the four-shell magazines into the shotgun.

There was a light rapping at my door: two long, one short. It was the right signal. Nevertheless, I took the shotgun with me when I unlocked the door.

"They're gone now," Crow said when he stepped inside. "Just faded away in the night. Reju's checking to make absolutely sure."

But if Crow was sure, they *were* gone. Nobody could teach him much about night stalking. Or day stalking, for that matter. In 'Nam he'd been the one in our squad who usually got stuck with the job of finding enemy snipers.

He had a troubled frown on his freckled, blunt-featured face as he watched me put the shotgun back in the bag. "I should've stuck closer to you,'' he growled. ''I was too far behind when I heard that shot.''

''I can get along without that *mea culpa* crap,'' I growled back. ''You were where I wanted you.''

His job was to tail me and check whether anybody else tried to, staying far enough back so he wouldn't be seen. Just as it had been Reju's job tonight to stay around the pensione and keep watch without being seen.

They had both flown to Venice, checking in well before I got there with their weapons and my own. Reju was there because I needed protection and that kind of work was how he made his living. I had his absolute assurance that he was charging me his special reduced-to-rock-bottom rate, reserved for only three people he considered to be his friends. Crow was there because everyone needs somebody who'll go down the line for him when he's caught between a rock and a hard place, and Crow and I had been doing that for each other for almost half of our lives.

Inside the pensione we made sure nobody saw we knew each other. Outside, they were supposed to keep their distance. Unless breaking cover became a matter of life or death. *My* life or death.

The idea was to get the gang used to thinking I was all alone in this town. Tonight should have done it, if they hadn't spotted Crow or Reju taking part.

I asked Crow about that. He shook his head. ''They didn't see *me*, that I guarantee. Hell, you could've been dead and buried by the time I finally got there.''

''Don't remind me.''

Crow managed his first grin. He got out a flask, unscrewed the cap, and handed it to me. Brandy. I took a long swallow. Then Crow had one. By the time Reju **arrived,** Crow was back to acting his lazily unflappable self.

''They *are* gone,'' Reju told us as he gave me back the little flashlight.

I put it on the table and asked him what I'd asked Crow. "You're sure none of them spotted you?"

"Positive. And the one in the canal—they'll think you did that." Reju took off his raincoat and folded it neatly over his arm. "No one to tell them different," he added. "I think I broke his neck. If I didn't, he's drowned by now."

Reju's tone and expression when he said that was exactly the same as when he'd told me how much Fritz's roses had cost him.

"The one that came down from the roof," Crow told me, "that could've been the guy Robby you described. Same kind of build."

Reju nodded, "He had a rifle with a sound suppressor and a night scope."

Crow looked at him under drooping eyelids and drawled, "Good thing Pete's a fast jumper. Another second and the bastard would've blown his head off."

"But I didn't intend to allow him all of that second," Reju said flatly. "I would have shot him before he steadied his aim." He looked mildly surprised that Crow didn't know that.

I went into the bathroom to check my bathwater. Perfect timing. Right temperature and depth. I took off the towel and settled into the tub. Crow came in, flipped down the toilet lid and sat down. Stretching out his legs, he handed me the flask again.

Reju appeared in the doorway as I had another belt. He leaned against the side of the door and studied his image in the mirror over the sink. He was the only one I had ever seen do that without changing expression the slightest.

I gave Crow back his flask and said, "I guess neither of you saw Isabelle Lachard tonight. Or I'd have heard about it by now."

"She wasn't there," Reju said positively.

Crow nodded agreement. "These were all men. Maybe your girl Isabelle left town."

Maybe so, but the next day she was back.

⊠ **29** ⊠

SHE CALLED THE PENSIONE AT NOON AND ASKED FOR ME. I was out having a quick lunch. She didn't leave her name, just a message that she would call again in an hour.

It was twelve-thirty when I got back to the pensione and learned about it. I settled down to wait for her call. It came at 1 P.M. On the dot.

"My name is Isabelle Lachard," she told me. "I understand you have been trying to get in touch with me. Could you tell me why?" Her voice was like her picture. Pleasant, and quiet.

"Sure," I said, "in person. Not over a phone."

There was a slight hesitation. Then she said, "I could meet you at three this afternoon. There is an *osteria* over by the . . ."

I cut her off. "Three is fine. But I pick the place."

"All right," she said. "Where?"

"Florian." That was as public a place as I could think of. Right on the Piazza San Marco. At three in the afternoon the café would be full of tourists and natives. With at least two pairs of cops strolling around the piazza just outside.

"All right," she said again. "Florian at three."

"I can wear a yellow carnation," I said.

"No need. I know what you look like."

171

I doubted that the baron's description would have been flattering. But probably accurate enough to identify me.

It was one-thirty when I set out for San Marco. A leisurely stroll and an hour of idling over a drink never hurt anybody. It also never hurts to arrive for that kind of appointment ahead of time. Before the enemy gets around to booby-trapping it.

The news prediction continued to prove accurate Venice was high and drying out. A strong afternoon sun was evaporating the last puddles. It made the air hazy above the canals and squares. Out over the lagoon the haze was denser, verging into patches of low fog. Nearby San Michele—the cemetery island where Venice took its dead—was as ethereal in the mist as its centuries of ghosts. Islands farther out on the lagoon couldn't be seen at all.

The haze also cut the heat of the sun. Coupled with a winter breeze that made the air cold enough to make almost everyone wear some kind of coat or windbreaker. My raincoat was not conspicuous.

I stopped off at the post office to place my long-distance phone call to Fritz. It would be too easy for someone to tap the line at the pensione.

Fritz came on the phone sounding pleased with life. His doctor had agreed to let him leave the hospital in two days. He'd already hired a home nurse to take care of him. If I knew Fritz, he'd picked the prettiest he could get.

I filled him in on my own adventures last night and told him what I was planning to do that afternoon.

Fritz said, "Be *very* careful, my boy."

I didn't need anybody else to tell me that. Leaving the post office, I became increasingly alert as I neared San Marco. The enemy could have decided to get there early, too. The fact that Crow and Reju were already there didn't mean I could relax a fraction. Having some outside protection is extra insurance. It's not a substitute for watching your own ass.

* * *

After his conquest of Italy, Napoleon said that the Piazza San Marco would make the grandest drawing room in Europe. He ran into some hard knocks after that and never got around to roofing it over. The sky remains its ceiling and everything else that makes it exciting is still there. The sheer spaciousness. The endless columns of its arcades and upper facades. The multidomed San Marco Basilica, adorned by the magnificent bronze horses the Venetians looted from Constantinople.

The pigeon convention, however, always seems to leave the most lasting impression. It's hard to cross the piazza without kicking some and getting others in your hair. They were there in the usual mobs that afternoon, in the air, on the ground, perched on every statue and windowsill.

The cops were there, too, patrolling in teams and looking like actors in their operetta uniforms. But the weapons they carried weren't stage props.

I didn't see Crow or Reju and didn't look around for them. They'd be there somewhere—at vantage points where they could watch the entrance of the Florian café under the southern arcade and see its front rooms through the lineup of tall windows.

There were a couple dozen people at the tables outside Florian. I didn't join them. An outside table would be the easiest place for Crow and Reju to keep watch over me. But it would also make me an exposed, stationary target for someone with a scoped rifle. Firing from a roof or upper window all the way across the piazza, the shooter could vanish well before the police made the climb and began searching.

I crossed the arcade and entered the café. Without stopping, I walked through its meandering succession of richly-decorated chambers to the men's room. Locking myself in, I took off my raincoat and unslung the shotgun hanging against my side. The shotgun's abbreviated barrel and pistol grip made it easy to conceal. I held it by the grip with the barrel pointing down, and draped the raincoat over it. It disappeared completely.

With that short a barrel the shotgun wasn't much good for anything but closeup work. But close up was what I had in mind. Even the fastest handgun expert can be scared off by a shotgun. The one holding it doesn't have to take dead aim, just swing it in the basic direction of the target. The handgun whiz can shoot you dead, and still get blasted if your finger pulls the trigger as you go down.

Leaving the men's room, I strolled back through the café. The first two front rooms near Florian's entrance were full up. But in the third I found what I wanted: a little corner table available by the window. Settling down on the red velvet banquette, I placed the raincoat-covered shotgun on my knees under the table's marble top. I made sure the raincoat didn't impede access to the trigger before the waiter came over.

The price of the cheapest nonalcoholic drink at Florian can uspet even customers used to the most expensive bars in the States. But—as in any café throughout Italy and France— what that price buys you is the table, for as long as you care to stay. I ordered a cappuccino.

There was almost a full hour to go before Isabelle Lachard was due. My corner position put my back to a wall paneled with Turkish scenes painted on glass. The panel behind me depicted erotic goings-on inside a harem. It was reflected in a large gilt-framed mirror on the other side of the narrow room, which also gave me an extended view down the Piazza San Marco toward the Clock Tower. Through the window beside me I could see directly across the piazza to the crowded tables outside the Quadri, Florian's major rival. I watched and waited.

My waiter returned with a foam-topped glass of cappuccino in a silver holder. I used my left hand to stir in two sugars and take a sip. My right hand was on my thigh under the table, touching the hidden shotgun. I continued to wait and watch.

She appeared at three o'clock. On the dot. Coming through the piazza from the direction of the basilica. I recognized her when she turned left toward Florian.

My first impression of Isabelle Lachard in person was that she moved like a cat. Not your tame house tabby. Think of one of the big cats in a zoo, pacing its cage just before feeding time. I could have been reading that into the way she moved, influenced by what I knew. But that's how it seemed to me.

Other than that she was like her picture. A rather nice-looking young woman with nothing striking about her except those straight, thick eyebrows that almost formed a single bar. She was on the short side, with a sturdy figure and strong legs. Her flat-heeled shoes didn't add much to her height. She was carrying a small embroidered purse. Her tweed coat was open over a plain white blouse and short plaid skirt.

I watched her pause for a swift scan of the outside tables and Florian's windows. Then she came on toward the entrance and disappeared from view for a few moments. She reappeared in the doorway of my room, glancing around it before coming over to stand before my table.

"Monsieur Sawyer?"

"Nice of you to join me, Mademoiselle Lachard." The instant I said it I saw the gold band on her wedding finger. But she didn't correct me by giving her married name.

She didn't sit down immediately. Instead, she put her cloth purse on my table and took off her coat. Then she turned away and walked over to the coat rack.

I put my hand on her purse. No weapon inside, not even a tiny one. I examined her sturdy figure while she was hanging up her coat and continued to when she turned around and came back toward me. The sleeves of her blouse clung to her arms and buttoned at her wrists. The hem of her skirt was above her knees. The only place she could be concealing a gun would be fastened high to the inside of one thigh.

I didn't think so. She walked with her legs too close together. And if she had a knife up her sleeve I couldn't spot it.

I relaxed a notch. Just one.

✣ **30** ✣

THE WAITER CAME OVER AS ISABELLE LACHARD SAT DOWN
across the table from me.

"My treat," I told her. "Take whatever you'd like."

She decided what she'd like was three scoops of vanilla
ice cream with strawberries on it and a tall glass of Vichy. I
ordered an Irish whiskey, no water or ice. When the waiter
went off, Isabelle Lachard folded her squarish hands together
on the table like a schoolgirl at her desk and asked, "Now,
Monsieur Sawyer, why were you looking for me?"

She had almost as little change of expression as Reju. But
her basic look wasn't dour. Just quietly thoughtful. The eyes
under her dark, thick brows were brown verging into hazel.
They watched me inquiringly. I couldn't detect the slightest
hint of menace in them.

"It's not really you I'm after," I said. "I'm hoping you'll
help me find somebody else. A man named Arnaud Galice."

"I don't know anybody of that name," she said.

"Maybe you know him by another name." I pointed to
the wedding ring she'd apparently removed each time before
visiting the baron. "Maybe you're even married to him." I
described Galice the way he looked now.

"No," she said evenly, "I don't know a man of that description. Why did you think I might?"

"For one thing," I told her, "Galice has always been good

177

at latching on to the right woman, to help him with whatever he needed to do. I imagine when you met him he was scared stiff that a gang of dope smugglers he'd stolen a shipment from might still be looking for him. He felt he needed some permanent protection. So he latched on to you.''

"I really don't understand what you're talking about,'' she told me. There was no emotion in the way she said it. "Perhaps if you would explain why *you* are searching for this man, it would help.''

"He shot my partner,'' I said. "Like Sam Spade explained, when somebody does that you're supposed to do something about it.''

"I'm not acquainted with this person you're quoting, Monsieur Sawyer. You become less comprehensible with every thing you say.'' Again, she didn't seem annoyed, simply making an editorial comment.

"Let's just pretend for the moment that I'm right about one thing: Arnaud Galice got you to fall for him. As I said, he's good at that—with plenty of others before you. He'd faked his death and changed his appearance. Plastic surgery, diet, wig. But he still didn't feel entirely safe from the people whose dope he stole. With somebody like you around he could feel much safer.''

The waiter brought our orders. Nothing Florian serves comes cheap, but they don't stint either. My Irish whiskey filled half of a good-sized glass. Her three balls of vanilla ice cream were covered by a generous portion of strawberries. I took a sip of the whiskey, let it slide down slowly, and put my glass back on our little table, savoring the strong after-taste.

Isabelle Lachard drank a little of her Vichy and got started on her dessert. Delicately, she scooped a single strawberry into her mouth, then fished under the others to spoon up some ice cream. She added that to the strawberry before chewing and swallowing. The taste made her smile, just a little.

I watched her as I resumed my story.

"But Galice finally began running low on the money from his dope sale. He couldn't go back to his former scams to make more because he would run into people who knew him too well. But he'd already begun preparing for the problem by making new kinds of contacts. With smugglers connected to the art underworld probably. And one of them told him about finding an Etruscan tomb. Hidden by a landslide a couple thousand years ago. Opened by another probably a year or two ago."

I couldn't see any reaction at all in her to what I was saying. She went on eating slowly but with obvious pleasure, with an occasional sip from her glass of Vichy.

"One problem with this tomb," I said. "From a thief's viewpoint, that is. It was empty, except for a few things almost impossible to steal without destroying them in the attempt. But Galice got an inspiration. He made contact with either Baron von Stehlik or Friedhelm Dollinger first. Whichever, that one introduced him to the other. Galice needed both. Von Stehlik for contacts with artisans who could fake Etruscan decorative arts for him. Dollinger for his connections with wealthy collectors that don't mind adding smuggled plunder to their collections."

I paused and said, "Interesting so far?"

"Not very," she told me blandly, "but perhaps it would be if I knew the people you're talking about."

I went on with it. "It must have taken at least a year to get all that stuff made. Then they planted it in the tomb. Since the tomb was authentic that would lend an apparent legitimacy to whatever was found in it. But Galice needed more than that to clinch it. So Dollinger contacted Susan Kape and got her interested. Galice knew she wouldn't buy until what he was selling was tested, and none of it would stand up under scientific analysis.

"But if *her* intention to buy became known, other big collectors—ones Galice got to know through Dollinger—

would leap in to grab it. So eager to beat her to the find that *they* wouldn't question its credentials. Because Galice wouldn't give them the time. He'd make it a fast take-it-or-forget-it proposition.''

I paused again and told her, "You're allowed to interrupt me at any point where you think I'm going wrong."

Isabelle Lachard shook her head. "No, please go on. I still don't understand why you're telling me all of this, but it is becoming interesting.''

I choked down a sudden desire to slug her because I couldn't seem to get a reaction any other way. Instead I tried doing it with words.

"As sting operations go, this one wasn't bad. Dollinger was a pretty sharp con artist, but it seems Galice is better. He made it a sting within a sting. But then it ran into unexpected complications. Because Susan Kape hired Fritz Donhoff, my partner. Carmen Haung warned Dollinger about it, and that night when Galice visited him, he told him. That scared Galice, because he and Fritz know each other. Galice knows me, too, but Carmen Haung had told Dollinger that Fritz hadn't been able to contact me about his new job yet.

"It was Fritz that worried Galice. Because Fritz could recognize him and spread the word he was still alive. So when he spotted Fritz tailing him away from Dollinger's that night, he panicked and shot him. It had to be sheer panic. Or he would have been a little more patient, taking the necessary time to bring *you* to Paris. To do a professional job of killing. The way he did afterward to clean up the messy results of his panic.''

She went on with her dessert, one strawberry and one spoon of vanilla ice cream at a time. Ninety percent of the girls I went to the University of Chicago with never managed to look that innocent.

"Paul Dupuy was conned into waiting in Fritz's place to kill me," I said. "He didn't have any connection with the sting operation. Galice paid him to do it so he could wind up as the dead sucker. Galice wasn't worried about me much, because I didn't know anything. You killed Dupuy to lay a false trail for the cops to follow. To protect your man.''

Isabelle Lachard ate the last of her dessert, picked up her napkin, and patted her lips delicately.

''Dollinger,'' I continued, ''was out of France by then. Probably took off right after Fritz was shot. Maybe he didn't even know about the shooting. What he did know was he was being investigated, and it was better for him not to be around. But that left his girlfriend, and maybe she knew a few things. Galice asked you to move her out, too. Only I showed up before you could. So you killed her. For the same reason you killed Dupuy—protecting your man from harm.''

She had another sip of Vichy, put down her glass, and folded her hands on the table again. Sitting back in her chair, she looked at me like a student listening to an uninspired lecturer.

''I don't think you murdered Dollinger,'' I said. ''Not your style of killing. Maybe you didn't even know it was in the cards. I'm sure von Stehlik didn't. He wouldn't have any part of something that scary. But it did achieve its objective. All that publicity about the fabulous treasure missing from that tomb. Galice must have rich collectors begging him for it by now. He can go for the highest bidder.''

That was it: the end of what I had to tell. I leaned against the back of the banquette and picked up my whiskey glass. It was still almost half full. I'd concentrated all my attention on watching for her reactions after my first sip. I made up for that now with a healthy swallow. Then I put down the glass and looked at her and waited.

After several moments she asked quietly, ''Is that all?''

''Uh-huh.''

''I assume that was a story you were making up? You didn't mention any proof of any of it.''

''I don't need proof,'' I told her. ''I'm not out to stop the con game, or to nail most of the people working it. Whoever winds up getting stung, paying out a fortune for what's supposed to be looted art, deserves the sting. I'm only interested in one thing. Having a talk with Arnaud Galice.''

''But I can't help you find him,'' Isabelle Lachard said. ''Since I don't know him.''

''Tell him,'' I said, ''that I've got everything I've just told you typed up. And in a safe place. It's rigged to get circulated if he doesn't get in touch with me in the next two days. That's the deadline. The same thing happens if I die or disappear. It includes a detailed description of what he looks like now. Among the people it goes to are those Turks he stole the heroin from. They won't fall for the same gag twice. They'll never stop hunting him this time. Tell Galice that.''

She looked at her watch and said, ''I'm sorry, but I really have to go now.''

''Sure.''

She drank the last of her Vichy, took her purse, and stood up. ''Thank you for the treat.''

''My pleasure.'' I watched her walk away toward the coat rack. My nerves tightened as I got a sudden prevision of her taking a gun out of her coat pocket and doing a fast turn with it aimed at me. I slid my finger across the trigger of the shotgun under my raincoat.

But all she did was put on the coat and walk out of the room without looking back at me.

After a few moments I saw her go out onto the Piazza San Marco, crossing it in the direction of the Clock Tower. She never once looked behind her. Galice would have assigned others to check on whether I tried to follow her.

I didn't try. That job was up to Crow and Reju. This was the point where my walking into last night's trap—apparently unaided—paid off. It would be *me* they'd be keeping tabs on.

Isabelle Lachard went under the arch of the Clock Tower and disappeared into the Merceria.

I finished my whiskey, paid the bill, and carried the raincoat-wrapped shotgun back to the men's room. After locking the door I hung the shotgun from my left shoulder, down between my arm and side. The men's room was stuffy. It seemed to me a place like Florian could afford to put in better air circulation than that. I put on the raincoat and walked out through the café in search of fresh air.

I was crossing the arcade outside Florian when it hit me all the way.

My vision suddenly blurred, and my brain tried to pressure its way out of the top of my skull. My balance went to hell. I stumbled and grabbed the back of a terrace chair to keep from falling. The haze in the piazza around me was becoming a dense fog, and its cold was racing through my veins, turning to ice.

The chair was unoccupied so I took it, clinging to the back for support until I managed to get seated. I knew I shouldn't just sit there like that. I should be making myself throw up and start yelling for help. But I couldn't seem to get any drive behind the thought. I was experiencing a bout of enervating euphoria that the situation didn't warrant.

It kept getting stronger. It didn't hurt, but my head was swimming and my legs weren't there. None of which kept me from knowing I'd been suckered.

I'd been thinking guns and knives. Concentrating on where she could have one concealed under her clothes. And all the time her weapon had been hidden between a couple of her fingers probably. Ready to be dropped into my whiskey one of the times she'd reached for her own drink.

I had been watching her the whole time. She'd done it *while* I was looking, and I hadn't seen it. Like a sleight-of-hand artist doing his magic act. Tricking you into thinking you were watching everything he was doing but you were missing the important part.

Reju had warned me: Isabelle Lachard was very good. And I'd been neatly conned. But I couldn't seem to get very worked up about it. I found myself watching San Marco swirl around me and thinking it was a hell of a beautiful place to die.

I began to tilt off the chair. Strong hands grabbed my shoulders and straightened me up.

An anxious voice was asking me in French, "What is the matter, Pierre-Ange, another attack?"

There was a face in the fog, looking down at me with frowning concern. A lean face with a short, pointy beard. The face swelled and shrank, dissolved and reappeared.

Other people around me. Worried Italian voices.

Arnaud Galice answering them in Italian. I registered detached bits of it. "I'm a doctor. . . . My friend is not supposed to drink. . . . Diabetic condition . . . We'll get him home and take care . . ."

Two other men, hauling me to me feet.

We were walking through the fog, with Galice leading the way. I found I *could* walk. It's easy, with a man on either side holding you up.

There was a stretch of oblivion and then a vague snatch of awareness. I was in a motorboat. Speeding through the mist across the lagoon. Arnaud Galice—the new Arnaud Galice of the lean face and dark hair and beard—was sitting beside me, preparing a hypodermic needle.

The mist darkened, and I went back to oblivion.

⊠ **31** ⊠

THERE WAS A MUSTY SMELL: DAMP EARTH AND DECAYING plaster. Outside that, less distinct, the smells of lagoon, marsh, and sea.

My mouth and throat felt like I'd drunk a pint of desert sand. My brain throbbed in tune with my pulse, but it was no longer filled with fog. I was stretched out on my back on what felt like a thin, bare mattress. I tried moving my arms. No problem with the right one, but the left was doubled above the top of my head, the wrist handcuffed to something. I moved my legs. Both of those were free.

A voice spoke in French. "Good. I thought you would awake about this time." Arnaud Galice.

I opened my eyes. There was a cracked, flaking ceiling above me, with a bare bulb that seemed to supply all the light there was. A feeble light, but it hurt my eyes. I squinted and turned my head. Galice sat in a plain wooden chair to my right, just beyond reach, one leg crossed over the other.

He glanced at his watch, uncrossed his legs, and said, "Where is this typed report about me that you claim to have made?"

My attempt at speech produced a noise like a rusty hinge. Galice stood up and walked away to a corner. I heard him turn on a water tap. I checked what I was lying on. The mattress was nothing more than a pad on a narrow metal-frame bed. The headrail my left wrist was cuffed to was only a couple inches higher than the mattress. The footrail was just as low.

Galice came back with a tin cup. I reached for it with my free right hand, but he didn't come that close. He put the cup down on the warped planks of the floor and stepped back.

"If you sit up you can reach it," he told me.

A wave of dizziness hit me when I sat up. Nothing like what had happened to me outside Florian, but enough to make me wait without moving farther until it passed. Then I swung my legs carefully off the bed and planted my feet on the floor. By pulling my cuffed left wrist along the headrail as far as I could, I was able to reach down with my right hand and pick up the tin cup. But bending down brought another wave of dizziness.

This one was slighter than the first and passed sooner. I sat up with the cup and gulped down all the cold water it held.

After a couple more tries I got my voice unhinged enough to croak, "More." I tossed the cup to him.

He grabbed for it with both hands, fumbled, but finally managed not to drop it. Galice had never been too skillful, except at inventing elaborate schemes and ensnaring susceptible women.

While he refilled the cup I took in my surroundings. The inner walls were of crumbling cinderblock. There was no window. The closed wooden door looked solid. My raincoat and jacket had been hung on one of the pegs near the door. On the wall beyond the foot of my bed there was a workbench, a couple plastic buckets, and a few garden tools. Judging by the cobwebs strung between them, they hadn't been used in a long time.

Galice brought the filled cup back and put it on the floor. I had to stretch down farther to reach it this time, but this time there was hardly any dizziness. "I could use some aspirin with this," I croaked. "I've got a headache."

"That will pass," Galice told me, moving the chair farther away and sitting down. "Though the drug *is* quite strong while it lasts. A most effective drug, as you discovered. And colorless, odorless, tasteless. Very useful."

It was odd, looking at that new face and hearing that remembered voice come out of it. But after you looked for a while you could still see it was Arnaud Galice. If you knew what you were looking for ahead of time. You wouldn't recognize him with a disinterested glance.

I emptied the cup again, and after that I could speak without croaking. "What time is it? Somebody's taken my watch."

"Serge—one of my associates—fancied that. It is a few minutes past eight."

That made it more than four hours since Isabelle Lachard left Florian. That worried me. The cavalry should have arrived before now.

"Where are we?"

"South of Venice," Galice said, "on the coast near the Brenta Canal. One of the old Veneto country estates, now somewhat dilapidated. I've been renting it for the past fourteen months. This used to be its garden shed."

He was being very free with information. Why not, he didn't expect me to go anywhere with it.

I watched him cross one leg over the other again, linking his hands around the raised knee. The hands were the only part of him that retained some of his former plumpness. "Now then, I don't really believe that document on me really exists, of course . . ."

"It exists," I told him flatly. I have some talent and experience at lying. The possibility that I was telling the truth gnawed at him.

"If it does," he said, "I want it. If it doesn't, I have to be certain it doesn't."

"Unlock these handcuffs and we'll talk about it."

"I couldn't unlock them if I wanted to," he told me. "I

don't have the keys at the moment. A small precaution. As for talking, I couldn't believe anything you told me at present. I'm afraid there's only one way I'll be able to believe what you say—after you've been through a considerable amount of pain. I'm really *very* sorry that is necessary.''

He did look sorry. That didn't mean it wasn't going to happen.

''The man you know as Robby is in charge of things like that,'' Galice added. ''He is something of a sadist, you see. But there is not enough time for that right now. We have an important visitor expected in an hour over at the house. And I don't think an hour will be long enough for even Robby to get the truth out of you. So that will have to wait until later.''

Later suited me. Later might be long enough. I said, ''Important visitor—that would be the sucker you finally fastened on to.''

Galice nodded and smiled at me, his sadness about being forced to have me tortured forgotten. ''Rasul Khdanni. His yacht should be anchoring off the coast nearby very soon.''

Maybe that was why Galice was spending a little time in my cell with me. Just to do some boasting about how big a fish he'd landed. He figured I was the only one outside his gang he could boast to safely.

I knew all about Rasul Khdanni. One of his properties was not far from my house on the Côte d'Azur. But everybody knew about Khdanni. He loved publicity about being one of the richest men in the world. He'd gotten that way by acting as a go-between in financial deals between western nations and the oil-fat Middle East. His mammoth yacht was a floating art museum. His penthouse duplex in New York and his mansions in Spain, England, Argentina, and Singapore were filled with more art. Old, sound-investment art. The kind that could be depended on for a profit-making resale in the future.

''Neat,'' I said. ''He takes the stuff out from here to his

yacht by motor launch and sails off. That way you don't even have the problem of smuggling it across a frontier.''

Galice nodded happily, pleased that I realized how clever he'd been.

"How much are you gouging him for that fake Etruscan junk?''

"Twenty-three million dollars," Galice told me with some awe. "Three million of it he's already transferred to my numbered account in Switzerland as down payment. Tonight he will arrange with his Swiss bank to transfer the remainder. By phone, when we give him the treasure.''

"You'll be a rich man, Arnaud. For a little while.''

"For a long time, I think." But Galice's new face had lost its happy smile. The menace always hovering over him was something he could never take lightly. Galice had the guts to make a daring play, but not to accept the consequences. "I'll have enough fortune after this to live well, very far away.''

"The Israelis found Eichmann," I told him. "The Turks will find you.''

Galice uncrossed his legs abruptly and got to his feet. "That we will discuss after Rasul Khdanni leaves. Again, I regret the means we will have to use.''

He crossed the room and opened the door. The feeble light from the room fell on rank growths of tall weeds outside. Two men stepped in.

One of them was Robby. He stopped just inside the door, looking at me with that genial, fat-man smile.

The other was taller than any of us and almost as big around as Robby, with beady little eyes in a sullen, bony face. He was carrying my shotgun in one large hand. What looked like my holstered pistol was clipped to his belt. Later I saw that the watch on his wrist was mine, too. Another collector.

Galice told him, "Be careful around him, Serge. Don't get too close. And give me back the key to the handcuffs.''

Serge dug a small key out of his pocket. Galice took it from him and walked out into the night.

Robby went on smiling at me for a moment. "See you later," he promised, and then followed Galice, shutting the door after him.

⊠ **32** ⊠

SERGE SETTLED HIS BULK ON THE CHAIR OUT OF MY REACH. He rested the stubby shotgun on one knee, pointing it at me.

I sat on the narrow metal-frame bed and looked at him for a while. He looked back at me without much expression. Finally I nodded at the cup on the floor. "Could you get me a drink of water?"

"No." That's all he said, flat and final.

I sat there with my head lowering, my face growing miserable. After a time I pressed my right forearm against my middle and bent lower. A few minutes more and I croaked, "I *need* some water. I feel sick—that dope they fed me."

This time Serge didn't answer at all. Just shrugged a heavy shoulder and continued to sit there impassively, his beady eyes and the big mouth of the shotgun watching me.

I lay back on the narrow bed, one forearm across my forehead and the other still against my middle, and waited.

I kept estimating the amount of passing time while I waited. Ten minutes . . . twenty minutes . . . When it got to half an hour, I decided I couldn't wait any longer.

Crow and Reju *could* have lost track of Isabelle Lachard. I knew Reju was pretty good at tailing anybody, and Crow was one of the best. But if they'd managed to stick with her all the way, they should be here. And they weren't. Outside protection was swell, when it was there. But it wasn't, and it *was* my ass.

I began collecting saliva in my mouth, working to not swallow any of it. When I had enough I rolled over on my side and made some sick noises. Serge didn't budge from the chair, but he was watching me with more interest now.

I gritted my teeth and moaned, "I'm going to vomit!"

Serge stayed put.

I rolled off the bed, hitting the floor on my knees and clutching at my stomach with my free hand. Making gagging noises and letting the saliva dribble out of my mouth.

Serge got up, carrying the shotgun in one hand, and hurried over to the workbench. I crawled behind the head of the bed, still gagging. He snatched up one of the cobwebbed buckets and turned and tossed it on the bed.

It bounced off the mattress as I shoved to my feet, grabbed the headrail with both hands, and ran the bed across the floor at him. The footrail rammed into his legs below the knees. He toppled over it and landed awkwardly on the mattress. I clouted him across the side of the neck with my right fist and all my strength behind it.

He was twisting away when it connected. It didn't put him out. But it did loosen his hold on the shotgun. I ripped it away from him, one-handed. Serge lurched up off the bed, grabbing for the holstered pistol. I used the shotgun as a club. The barrel slugged him across the throat.

He thudded to the floor. His arms and legs thrashed spasmodically for a few seconds and then relaxed. I didn't have to look to know that was all for Serge. The sound of breakage when the shotgun clubbed his throat had already told me that.

I dragged the bed over to the workbench with my handcuffed left hand. There was a metal cabinet at the back of the workbench. I searched it. There was nothing in it I could use to pick the handcuff lock. But I found something else: a pair of pliers and a screwdriver.

I sat down on the floor, facing the door. Placing the shotgun close to hand, I began working to unscrew the cap nut from the first of the four bolts attaching the metal headrail to the bedframe. It wasn't easy, with one wrist attached to the headrail. The threads were clogged with paint and rust.

But I got the first bolt off. I was starting on the second when somebody turned the outside door handle.

I dropped the tools and snatched up the shotgun. It was aimed at the door when Crow came in through it, swinging his Smith & Wesson .38 in a fast arc, ready to deal with the opposition.

When he saw the opposition sprawled on the floor, he shut the door and came over to study my predicament with the handcuffs. Holstering his revolver in the shoulder rig under his opened lumber jacket, Crow hunched down beside me, picking up the pliers and screwdriver. In that position you could see the pommel of his hunting knife, sheathed inside his left boot.

I kept the shotgun trained on the door. "You took your time getting here."

"We ran into a problem tailing her," Crow explained while he worked at the second bolt. "She took a water-taxi near the Rialto Bridge. Wasn't another single motorboat left there for Reju and me to grab. By the time one came along, your Isabelle Lachard was long gone."

He stopped talking and applied all the pressure he could on the cap nut. It broke free of the paint with a sharp crack. Crow began the job of twisting it through the rusted threads as he resumed.

"We did get the name on the boat she took off in. But no guarantee it would come back to the same place. So Reju and me divided up the job. He took the second taxi and went off to look for hers at all the other landings around Venice."

"There's one hell of a lot of them."

"That's for sure. I stayed put at the Rialto landing in case the boat she'd gone off in did come back there. And it did. Two hours later, and Reju still hadn't come back. I forked out almost all my cash to get the driver to tell me where he took her and to bring me here.''

"What about Reju?" I asked Crow.

"Damned if I know. I had the water-taxi take me to the Riva near our pensione first. Left a message for Reju there, explaining where this place is. Hope he got it by now.''

I didn't bother pointing out that if Reju hadn't gotten it well before now, he wasn't going to get here on time to be of any help. Crow knew that. I watched him exert a final hard twist to the nut. It came off.

"The shoreline of this estate's all overgrown," he said while he began forcing the bolt out of its rusted hole. "Except right around its boat dock. I came ashore out of sight of the dock and reconnoitered. Big estate. But full of bushes and weeds gone wild. Easy to move around in. I saw a couple guys leave here for the big house. But then I had another little problem. A guy patrolling this area.''

"He still out there?"

"Uh-huh. But not a problem anymore." Crow pulled the bolt out. That left the two holding the other end of the headrail to the bedframe. But those didn't have to be removed.

Crow stood up and seized the headrail with both hands and pressed his foot against the frame. That pulled my end of the rail an inch away from the frame. I slid the attaching cuff down the rail to where it became one leg of the bed. Crow raised the bed off the floor, and I pulled the cuff free.

That left me with the cuffs dangling from my left wrist. But that wouldn't interfere much. I had the use of both hands again.

I took my holstered pistol off Serge and clipped it back on my belt while Crow told me about the layout of the estate. Swiftly but with all the vital details. Crow and I learned to work enemy territory in tandem way back in 'Nam.

He told me about the main house. "Big. A lot of rooms that aren't used. We could get in through there, if that's what you want.''

"If that's where Galice is," I said, taking my watch off Serge's wrist and strapping it on my own. "I want *him*."

Crow nodded. "There's a gunman doing sentry turns outside the house. We'll have to get past him first."

I picked up the shotgun. "Let's go."

⊠ **33** ⊠

HALFWAY ALONG THE SHORELINE OF THE BIG ESTATE THERE was a small cove. That was where Crow had told me the boat dock was sheltered. The garden shed behind us was north of the cove. The house was south of it, on a slight hill looking out over the dark lagoon toward the sandbar that separated lagoon from sea. The thin path Crow and I followed at first had been made by the trampling down of underbrush beneath groves of untended willows and olive trees.

It brought us to a bend midway along a much wider graveled path. The dock was out of sight at one end of it and the other end led toward the house, hidden behind the trees. I followed Crow across this path and into a cypress grove on the other side. We were pushing through a tangle of weeds there when we heard the sound of a boat approaching the dock. Heavy twin engines.

I touched Crow's shoulder and motioned for him to stay where he was. In the shadowy darkness between the trees I had to put my hand near his face for him to make out the signal. Leaving him there, I went back the way we'd come. When I could see the wide path from the dock I stopped with my right shoulder touching the thick trunk of a cypress. The sky had clouded over, and little moonlight came through. By standing still I became part of the tree.

Some six minutes later four men came along the path,

196

going in the direction of the house. Three of them carried flashlights aimed down at the path. It was impossible to make out their faces. But the build of the man leading the way was unmistakable: Robby. Behind him two men walked side by side, one of medium height and lean, the other short and fat. A taller, lean man brought up the rear.

The short, fat man was the one not carrying a flashlight. The figure fitted Rasul Khdanni. I'd seen him around Monte Carlo and often enough in the media. Usually with at least one slim young beauty who towered over him. The two lean men had to be his bodyguards. They'd been close by Khdanni the times I'd seen him in person. Tough former French paratroopers.

When they vanished around the bend in the path, I returned to Crow. Keeping my voice low, I told him what I'd seen.

He kept his voice just as low. "The bodyguards being there in the house could be an extra problem. If they think we're a threat to their boss."

"Or they could be some help," I said. "We'll see. If it looks wrong, we'll wait till they've gone."

We went on through the cypress grove. When we emerged from it, we turned to the right. Crow led the way up a slope through a vineyard that had long been allowed to grow wild. At the top of the slope was what had once been a vast garden terrace. The garden had become a disordered wilderness of overgrown bushes, tangles of wild vines and chest-high weeds.

Beyond that was the house.

It was a three-story villa in the Palladian style favored by noble Veneto families of the eighteenth century. Its long facade, now half-covered by unkempt ivy, was topped by the typical statues and florid chimneys. The centerpiece was the usual: a wide stone stairway rising to the second-floor entrance under a portico supported by four Corinthian columns.

Interior lighting showed through two of the small top-floor windows to the right of the portico, and from one of the tall, slender bottom-floor windows on the same side. But along the right wing's second floor, all of the big square windows were lit.

In the villa's left wing, however, all the windows were dark.

Crouching, we angled across the terrace toward the far corner of the dark left wing. As far as we could, we kept to the cover of the overgrown shrubbery. It ended too soon. There was a wide cleared space all around the villa.

Crow had warned me about that. And about the unpredictable timing of the exterior gunman's sentry rounds. He patrolled irregularly: there was no way to be sure when he'd step out of the shadows close by. He sometimes doubled back unexpectedly. And he had an assault rifle that was probably set for full automatic bursts. A problem.

There was a place in the clearing nearby where a couple short hedges that had been hacked down had begun to grow back in high, disorderly clumps. Crow touched my arm and pointed at it. Then he held three spread fingers up near my eyes.

We looked at the luminous dials of our watches at the same time, registering the exact minute and second. Then I did a fast crawl away from our cover. Crow stayed put, ready to shoot if the gunman on sentry patrol showed in time to spot me.

But the sentry still hadn't appeared when I reached the hedges. I went flat and snaked under them, and then tried to merge into the dark ground there. I put the shotgun down to leave both hands free. If I had to shoot a gun now, everything would be loused up.

I waited.

The gunman appeared as silently and unexpectedly as Crow had warned. He was suddenly there, stepping out of the shadows less than twenty feet from my hiding place, coming from the direction of the portico. My watch showed two minutes and forty seconds elapsed since Crow and I had coordinated. Not enough.

He went past me, very quiet on his feet. Carrying the assault rifle in both hands, ready for use. A mean weapon, on full auto: the best can spray a thirty-shot burst in three seconds.

He went out of sight around the corner of the left wing. If he continued on and circled the villa, he wouldn't come this way again for some five more minutes.

Instead he did one of his unpredictable turnabouts, reappearing from around the end of the left wing. My watch now showed almost four minutes elapsed since I'd parted from Crow. He'd signaled that any time after three minutes would do. I watched the sentry prowl back toward the portico, following a new route that took him between my hedges and the villa, but closer to the building.

He was a few steps past my position when I rustled a hedge branch.

The sentry stopped on a dime and spun with the assault rifle, looking back and forth swiftly, not'sure where the sound had come from. I rustled the branch again. Just a very little, enough to hold his attention but not enough to provoke an instant burst from his weapon. He took a step toward me. Aiming at the hedge hiding me but withholding fire. If he started firing, everybody would come pouring out of the villa. Then if it turned out to only be a field rat in the hedges, they'd all be mad at him.

He came closer, starting to circle my hiding place. I held my breath.

Crow rose up from the ground a little behind the gunman and to his right. I hadn't known where he was, hadn't seen him get there. He took two, long fast strides and hammered the butt of his .38 against the mastoid bone behind the sentry's right ear. I heard the impact—not a pleasant sound, but it wouldn't carry any distance beyond me.

I shot out from under the hedges fast enough to grab the assault rifle as it spilled from the sentry's hands. Crow had both arms locked around the guy's chest, holding him up. I put the weapon down silently on the ground and then helped Crow carry the limp body over into wild bushes of the garden terrace.

We left him hidden there and went back to the patch of hedge. I got my shotgun. Crow picked up the assault rifle. I gestured at the hedge, but he shook his head. I watched him work the change lever, switching the weapon from automatic to single-shot fire. He took it with him as we went around the corner of the villa's left wing.

Crow felt surer of himself with that than he had with the revolver, I knew. As a handgun shooter he was okay. But with a rifle he was one of the best marksmen I'd ever met.

The windows along the left side of the villa were all dark. Crow tried the first while I tried the second. Both were locked. Crow started past me to try the next one. I stopped him and pointed down at his boot. He took his hunting knife out of it and gave it to me.

I dug the knife into the wood between the window's meeting rails, working it back and forth until I'd made a hole deep enough for the point to reach the inside lock. A little more digging and I was able to use the knife point to flick open the lock. I gave the knife back to Crow and slid the lower sash up.

We climbed inside.

It took a long time, feeling our way through dark rooms and corridors, before we came to a narrow stairway leading up to the next floor. Since up there was where we'd seen most of the right wing's windows lighted, we climbed the stairs.

It was just as dark and silent up there. We worked our way toward the villa's right wing through more dark rooms. These were overcrowded with furniture, and we had to move carefully to make sure we didn't knock anything over.

We reached a corridor that ran from the front of the building toward the rear. Some electric lighting filtered into it from two sources: a second corridor off to our right and a third to our left. Both of those angled away in the direction of the right wing.

I gestured to Crow. He went off silently into the corridor to the right, leading the way with his newly acquired rifle.

I entered the other corridor. It led past narrow openings: a dark stairway to the top floor, open doors to even darker rooms. I paused and listened before stepping quietly past each dark opening. No sound inside any of them. I moved on with my stubby shotgun held at the ready in both hands, my finger reaching lightly across its trigger. The source of light was outside the other end of the corridor. It grew stronger as I neared it.

When I reached the end of the corridor, I stopped again to listen and let my eyes finish adjusting to the light streaming in there. I could hear voices, somewhere farther ahead. Somewhat muffled. I wasn't near enough to make out what was being said. I eased forward just sufficiently to see what was outside that end of the corridor.

It was a large rotunda forming a central hall whose curved walls rose through the upper story to a domed ceiling. The terrazzo floor gleamed like marble under the light of a big, gaudy Murano chandelier hanging halfway down from the dome. The flowered wallpaper was in sad condition: flaps of it hanging in places, exposing more layers of wallpaper and cracked plaster underneath.

Across the rotunda from me there was a low, curtained archway to the left and an identical one to the right. The closed curtains were of faded blue velvet that had nourished generations of moths. The muffled voices I heard came through those curtains.

There was no one inside the rotunda, as far as I could see

from my position at the end of the corridor. But part of the rotunda, off to my left outside the corridor, was blocked from my view by the back of a stairway rising to the top floor.

I stepped out of the corridor, looking in that direction. Two long strides took me past the back of the stairway. Nobody was on it. Beyond it there was only a closed door flanked by two decrepit leather armchairs. The stairs didn't lead to anything now. There'd been a doorway at the top, but it had been bricked up.

I crossed the rotunda silently, angling over toward the velvet-curtained archway to the left. When I reached it, I stopped and listened again. That close I could make out what was being said on the other side of the curtains.

The voice I heard at that moment was speaking in French. But it was unmistakably Aldo's, and now that I knew about his background I could detect the lecturing tone of the tourist guide in it.

". . . the goddess of Fate," he was saying. "Note what she holds in her hands. The inkwell and the stylus. To record her decisions on the destiny of each of us . . ." I remembered Aldo giving me the same lecture, almost word for word, in the Etruscan tomb.

I leaned forward slightly and put one eye to a little gap in the velvet where the two halves of closed curtain met. Another Murano chandelier lighted the big room on the other side. It had probably been a drawing room, but the only furniture in it now was a large round table with a telephone on it. The rest of the table, and much of the terrazzo floor, was cluttered with counterfeit Etruscan treasure. All of the objects I'd seen in the two chambers of the tomb.

There were five men in the room. There was Aldo and there was Galice. The other three were Rasul Khdanni and his lean bodyguards, the tall one and the medium-sized one. Aldo was going on about the bronze statue of the goddess, which stood on the floor at the other end of the room, beside a narrow open stairway leading up to a small balcony. But

Khdanni was waddling away from it to admire the gold pectoral, leaning against the wall on the other side of the stairs.

The bodyguards moved with Khdanni, as though attached by invisible wires, and flanked him when he stopped. Arnaud Galice stood in the middle of the room, smiling benevolently at his sucker.

There was a door up on the small balcony. It was open, and I couldn't see anything but murky darkness inside it. That bothered me. Because I didn't know where Robby was and, more important, I had no idea where Isabelle Lachard was.

Arnaud Galice interrupted Aldo's lecture, addressing Rasul Khdanni. "The gold and silver objects—and those of bronze—are, of course, the most immediately eye-catching. But all of this earthenware, one should remember, is equally valuable. Artistically and historically. When you consider the incredible quantity of it we have here. As well as the quality and exceptionally fine condition of its decorative work."

Khdanni continued to be enthralled with the gold pectoral, stooping to run chubby fingers over the rows of little figures embossed on it.

Galice strolled in my direction, stopping when he reached the big round table, gesturing at the painted earthenware amphoras, mixing jugs, and pitchers on it.

"All of these are treasures that match the best that any museum has." Galice's face in profile achieved something close to reverence as he reached out and barely touched a large mixing jar painted with a scene of gods mingling with sea serpents. "This *celebe* alone would bring a small fortune. The delicacy of the—"

"You don't have to continue the sales talk," Khdanni told him drily. "We're rather beyond my needing to be persuaded by now."

"In that case . . ." Galice came farther around the table, to where the telephone was. He patted it lightly. "Since you have now examined everything and made sure it is all here . . .'' He was looking toward Khdanni at the far end of the room, with his back to me now so I could no longer read his expression. But his tone had become crisp, businesslike. "Isn't it time for us to *complete* our transaction?''

I pushed through the velvet curtains into the room with them.

⊠ **34** ⊠

I WOULD HAVE PREFERRED TO WAIT UNTIL CROW GOT THERE, and until I knew where Isabelle Lachard was.

But the positioning of the men in the room—and of Arnaud Galice especially—was too perfect at that moment for me to let it pass.

And if I handled it just right, I had a chance to get Khdanni's bodyguards siding with me before Isabelle Lachard showed. I could use that kind of help in the absence of Reju.

I took two long steps inside the room and pressed the muzzle of the shotgun into the small of Galice's back. He jerked and then froze in position as I announced, loud and fast, "This is a shotgun jammed against your back, Galice. Shell in the chamber, ready to shoot."

I hoped it was loud enough for Isabelle Lachard to hear, wherever she was in the house. I wanted her too worried about the life of her man to make any hasty move against me.

Galice didn't budge, and neither did Khdanni. But the other three in the room did, very quickly.

Aldo threw himself facedown on the floor and stayed that way, with his hands cradling the back of his head.

Khdanni's bodyguards converged in front of their boss, blocking him from my view. In the same instant they whipped out identical revolvers with four-inch barrels: .357 Magnums, from the size of the muzzles pointing my way.

I had Galice between me and those muzzles. But I'm too large for somebody like Galice to hide all of me. And the bodyguards were probably good enough to shoot the parts of me that showed. But they held back on trying, because they didn't understand what was going on yet and so far I wasn't posing a direct threat to Khdanni, just to Galice.

I used their moment of hesitation, keeping it loud and fast and very polite. "Monsieur Khdanni, please tell your men not to shoot. I'm not here to harm you, I'm here to *save* you—from being swindled. Everything in this room is a fake."

"That's a lie!" Galice bleated.

"Shut up," I snarled at him. "It's true, and I can prove it."

Rasul Khdanni sidestepped out from behind the taller bodyguard, just enough to see me. Whatever his defects of character—and those were many in my book—they did not include faintheartedness. He didn't look scared at all, just curious.

His tall bodyguard growled at him, "For God's sake, monsieur, get back out of his line of fire!" He grabbed at his boss with his free hand and tried to shove him behind him again.

Khdanni slapped his hand away. "He is not aiming at *me*. Wait, both of you, until somebody does."

I used the diversion to change position a little. I didn't like that dark balcony doorway or the curtained archway to my right, but at least I could keep watch on them. It was the curtained archway behind me that worried me more. Keeping the shotgun against Galice's back with my right hand, I seized the back of his jacket with my left and shifted us both around the table until I had my back toward a blank wall. From that position I could watch both curtained archways, plus that door up on the balcony.

"You claim all of these pieces are forgeries?" Khdanni said.

"Junk," I said. "Expensive junk."

"But Etruscan experts have authenticated—"

"They said the *tomb* was authentic," I interrupted. "And the three pieces that were tested—only three—didn't come from that tomb. Galice and his gang bought them somewhere else. This stuff is all imitation. That's why he's selling it to you instead of Susan Kape. Because she intended to have it all tested before paying for it.

"There's the phone," I added. "All you have to do is call and ask her if that's true."

"Monsieur Khdanni," Galice blurted in a trembly voice, "this man is acting as an agent for Susan Kape!" He was not the bravest of men, physically, but he had too much at stake here not to make a try at saving it. "He's only trying to keep you from taking all this treasure instead of *her*!"

Robby came in through the curtained archway off to the right.

He came in with his hands locked together behind his neck and without his genial smile. Crow stepped in after Robby, prodding him with the rifle. He flashed me a lazy grin. "Spotted this one trying to sneak in on you, old buddy."

"Hold it," I snapped at the bodyguards. "The man with the rifle is my friend. Helping me stop this swindle."

The tall bodyguard had swung his Magnum to cover Robby and Crow. The other kept his pointed toward Galice and me. Khdanni told them quietly, "Don't shoot anyone until I decide *who* to shoot."

My smooth line of chatter hadn't won them over yet.

Galice spoke to him in a dead-reasonable tone. "What I said is true. It can be verified easily enough. This man's name is Sawyer, and you'll learn he does work for Susan Kape."

Khdanni frowned a bit. "Sawyer, that is a name familiar to me."

"It should be," I told him. "You've been trying hard enough to add my house to your property near Cap d'Ail."

"Ah, you are that one . . ." He began to smile. "I have learned quite a bit about you, Monsieur Sawyer. Including the fact that it is not your house. It belongs to your mother. But so far you've been able to persuade her not to sell to my agent."

"And I'm going to go right on persuading. You'll never get that house."

"So, we are enemies. But perhaps not in this matter." Khdanni looked down at Aldo, who was still on the floor. Sitting there now, with his scrawny arms wrapped around his knees and his eyes shut, leaning the side of his head against the goddess of Fate. With his toe, Khdanni nudged Aldo's hip. "And you, monsieur, what do you have to say? Is all this genuine, or a sham?"

Aldo straightened his head and opened his eyes. He looked toward Galice and me, then over at Crow and Robby. Finally he looked up at Khdanni, but couldn't meet his eyes.

"I can't say anything," he whispered miserably. "I don't want to be killed."

He didn't say which of us he was afraid would kill him. I watched Aldo press his head against the bronze goddess again, looking as if he was going to sleep there. He hadn't been young when I'd met him in Rome, but he'd aged a decade in the last few minutes.

Keeping the shotgun pressed against Galice's spine, I reached out with my left hand and picked up the big piece of painted pottery Galice had praised so warmly. "Worth a small fortune?" I let go of it. Khdanni winced visibly when it shattered on the floor.

I picked up an amphora and tossed it aside. This time Khdanni just watched with an interested look on his pudgy face when it crashed.

"I can keep that up," I said. "I can break up all the metal

junk with a hammer, too. If that's what it takes to persuade you Susan Kape wouldn't want any of it.''

Khdanni looked from the shattered pieces to Galice. ''I think I will have some of this tested before completing our transaction. And make that call to Susan Kape.''

''The deal is off!'' Galice shouted at him, his voice gone hoarse. ''I'll sell to somebody else! I've got no shortage of buyers!''

Khdanni told his bodyguards quietly, ''Watch the noisy gentleman and his associate. Don't let them do anything foolish while I—''

The lights blinked off, plunging the room into darkness.

What worried me most in that first second of total darkness was that open doorway up on the balcony. I had a vision of her coming down from there, knowing where I was . . .

The point was to not be there. To shift before anyone's eyes became adjusted to the dark. I locked my left arm around Galice's neck and pressed the shotgun harder against the small of his back.

''Move with me,'' I whispered close to his ear, ''or you're dead.''

I moved him toward the curtained archway nearest to me. I could see the lights in the rotunda outside had gone off, too. I shoved Galice ahead of me through the curtains. If she was waiting on the other side, she wouldn't do anything that might hurt her man instead of me. In the darkness she couldn't be sure.

As soon as we were through the curtains I dragged Galice to my right, sliding my back along the curving wall. Then I stopped, waiting and listening, with the curved wall at my back and Galice held in front of me. He was breathing harshly, making it hard to hear anything else. I couldn't see anything except the vague general shape of the rotunda.

I moved farther on around the curved wall, keeping Galice as my shield, with the shotgun against his spine just above his hips. I moved slowly. So did time. The dark was motionless, heavy, almost solid.

And then the lights snapped on again.

I squinted against the sudden glare and tightened my grip on Galice. There was nobody else in the rotunda. I was where I could see all the ways in and out of the rotunda except one. I could see the closed door between the seedy armchairs and both curtained archways.

What I couldn't see from my position was behind the stairway to the bricked-up door above: the dark corridor I had come out of the first time I'd entered the rotunda.

Crow came through the curtained archway farthest from me. He still had Robby in front of him, prodding him forward with the rifle. But I knew that even Robby's large body wouldn't be enough of a shield, if Isabelle Lachard was inside the dark corridor directly across the rotunda from Crow.

She was.

My shouted warning wasn't fast enough to make Crow jump back through the curtains in time. Even that might not have been enough. A gun cracked from inside the corridor I couldn't see. The bullet passed between Robby's legs and hammered into Crow's thigh.

The shock of it flung Crow sideways against the wall beside the archway, knocking the rifle loose from his grasp and sending it skidding away across the glassy smoothness of the terrazzo flooring.

I yelled, "Shoot again and I kill your man, Isabelle!"

Crow slid down the wall and sat on the floor, gritting his teeth and gripping his thigh with both hands, digging in his thumbs to slow the bleeding.

Robby turned to go after the rifle.

"One more step," I warned him, "and I'll blast your head off."

He stopped and turned back and saw the snout of my shotgun jutting out past Galice's waist, aimed at him. Galice wasn't about to try grabbing for it. First of all it wasn't his style. And my hold around his neck had him bent backward in a tight bow, looking up at the dome above, concentrating totally on fighting to get breath through his strangled throat.

Isabelle Lachard's voice sounded again. "Sit down on the floor, Robby, and then don't move again."

Robby looked toward the corridor behind the stairway with a puzzled scowl.

"Sit *down*," she repeated, this time with a master sergeant's authoritative bite in her voice.

Though I still couldn't see her because of the staircase, she must have stepped out of the corridor. Because Robby's change of expression said that *he* saw her—with her gun aimed at him. He lowered himself sullenly to the floor.

"You see, Monsieur Sawyer," she called from behind the stairway, "I don't want any complications. I want it kept simple. A simple exchange—my husband for this man I heard you call your friend."

I wondered where she'd been when she'd heard me say it: inside that balcony door or on this side of one of the curtained archways.

"I'm aiming at your friend's forehead this time," she called, "not his leg." Her voice was much like it had been in the café, just louder.

"And I've got the muzzle of this shotgun dug into your husband's spine again," I called back. "I've got the trigger depressed within a hair of firing. You could come out fast enough to shoot me dead, and he'd still get blown in half."

"He's telling the truth, Isabelle!" Galice cried. "You've got to make a deal with him—no tricks. Just get me out of this!"

"I'm coming out," she called. "Don't hurt Arnaud, and I won't shoot."

Isabelle Lachard stepped out from behind the stairway. Just one step. Holding a target pistol aimed across the rotunda, past Robby, at Crow's head. Crow looked back steadily, giving her his small poker smile.

She flicked a glance toward Galice and me without altering the aim of the pistol in her hand one fraction.

If I'd been holding any other kind of gun on her man, I'm sure she would have bet his life on her fast and fancy shooting. Her first bullet would have killed me and knocked me away from Galice at the same time. Even if my dying finger jerked the trigger, there'd be only a minimal chance of his getting killed by the shot. Nothing is more unpredictable than a dead man's bullet. But they usually miss what they were originally aimed at, or inflict a nonfatal wound.

A shotgun reverses those odds. Dead and falling away from him with that, if my reflex triggered it the spreading load of buckshot would tear her man apart.

So she didn't make the try. Her eyes returned to Crow. Her target pistol had never left him.

"Isabelle!" Galice cried out desperately. "Get me *out* of this!"

Isabelle Lachard said, "Let Arnaud go, Monsieur Sawyer. I want him to walk over here and into the corridor behind me. When he's safe in there, I'll back in after him. I give you my word I won't hurt your friend before I—"

A voice sounded behind the stairway in back of her. "Throw your gun away, mademoiselle. Carefully."

It sounded like Khdanni's tall bodyguard.

Keeping her pistol trained on Crow, Isabelle Lachard turned her head and looked behind her. He had to have the Magnum aimed at her, because she didn't try to turn the rest of her. "Don't be foolish," she said quietly, "we're on the same side. These other men are Monsieur Khdanni's enemies."

"That is for Monsieur Khdanni to decide, mademoiselle. Until then, no more guns. Throw it down."

She shrugged, lowering the pistol, and let it fall to the floor. Dropping her arms to her sides, she turned toward the bodyguard and said, "You really don't understand why these men came here, but it will be all right as long as you also make sure . . ." As she spoke in that quiet, relaxed tone, she sauntered behind the staircase to him.

She did it so casually and unexpectedly that she was out of sight with him before I could even start a warning. There was a long moment, and then the tall bodyguard tottered out into the rotunda, with his hands empty and the hilt of a knife protruding from his solar plexus.

He made a staggering half turn, looking in my general direction with a slightly perplexed expression. His hands fumbled upward and found the hilt of the knife. He clutched it and began pulling the blade out. He almost had it done when he toppled forward and his face struck the floor.

Robby did a swift roll across the floor and scooped up the target pistol Isabelle Lachard had thrown down. I shoved Arnaud Galice out of my way. Robby was coming up off the floor trying to get the pistol aimed at me when I fired the shotgun. It sounded like a small cannon going off inside the rotunda. A couple crystals dropped from the Murano chandelier and smashed on the floor.

The load of shot caught Robby in the chest, lifted him off his feet, and threw him away. He must have been finished before he fell, but the target pistol was still in his hand. It went off when he hit the floor.

I heard a soft grunt near me and turned my head. The bullet from the pistol had gone into Galice's left cheek, drilling upward. He turned very slowly on buckling legs and his convulsing fingers dug into loosened layers of wallpaper. He dragged thick folds of it down with him, settling on his spread knees with the crown of his head wedged against the base of the wall.

I cursed silently but viciously and aimed the shotgun toward the stairway that hid Isabelle Lachard. "I'm aiming at your husband again!" I yelled. She couldn't have seen what had happened to him from there.

"Watch it, Pete," Crow said through his clenched teeth. "She's got that Magnum now."

"I don't *want* to use it," she called. "You've got to make the exchange, Monsieur Sawyer. Arnaud for—"

She stopped talking when Jean-Marie Reju stepped through the curtained archway next to Crow with the big Colt .45 in his hand.

After a moment she said so softly I almost didn't hear it, *"You?"*

"Isabelle," Reju said in a dead-flat voice, "please don't force it. Just lower that—"

It sounded like one very loud gunshot. But it was the two of them, blending together: the Colt and the Magnum.

The bullet from the Magnum ripped the left sleeve of Reju's jacket and thudded into the wall behind him.

After a beat Reju lowered his gun.

I didn't have to look behind the stairway to know that Isabelle Lachard was dead.

And I didn't want to.

⊠ 35 ⊠

WE TOOK CROW TO THE HOSPITAL IN VENICE USING RASUL Khdanni's motorboat. Aldo vanished while we were occupied with that, and nobody really cared much about catching him.

Crow's wound wasn't as serious as it had looked at first. No bones broken. One blood transfusion and three days in the hospital, and they released him into the care of Reju and me. We took him home to his wife, Nathalie.

She didn't talk to me for almost three months after that. But I knew she'd get over her mad. She and I had been friends since we were kids, and you don't drop that kind of friendship over an unfortunate accident like getting her husband shot.

Rasul Khdanni never got his three-million-dollar down payment back. There was no way to pry it out of Arnaud Galice's numbered account without the right code word. Known only to Galice, and he was far beyond telling.

I went up to Paris to see how Fritz was getting along. He was getting along fine; the nurse *was* pretty.

I didn't tell anyone else besides him about Carmen Haung's part in the Etruscan swindle, because I couldn't think of any reason why I should.

And I never saw Susan Kape again. I decided I'm not up to anything that dangerous.